KNIGHT, HEIR, PRINCE

(OF CROWNS AND GLORY--BOOK 3)

MORGAN RICE

Books by Morgan Rice

THE WAY OF STEEL
ONLY THE WORTHY (BOOK #1)

VAMPIRE, FALLEN
BEFORE DAWN (BOOK #1)

OF CROWNS AND GLORY
SLAVE, WARRIOR, QUEEN (BOOK #1)
ROGUE, PRISONER, PRINCESS (BOOK #2)
KNIGHT, HEIR, PRINCE (BOOK #3)
REBEL, PAWN, KING (BOOK #4)

KINGS AND SORCERERS
RISE OF THE DRAGONS
RISE OF THE VALIANT
THE WEIGHT OF HONOR
A FORGE OF VALOR
A REALM OF SHADOWS
NIGHT OF THE BOLD

THE SORCERER'S RING
A QUEST OF HEROES
A MARCH OF KINGS
A FATE OF DRAGONS
A CRY OF HONOR
A VOW OF GLORY
A CHARGE OF VALOR
A RITE OF SWORDS
A GRANT OF ARMS
A SKY OF SPELLS
A SEA OF SHIELDS
A REIGN OF STEEL
A LAND OF FIRE
A RULE OF QUEENS
AN OATH OF BROTHERS
A DREAM OF MORTALS
A JOUST OF KNIGHTS
THE GIFT OF BATTLE

CHAPTER ONE

Even without every noble in Delos staring at him, Thanos would have felt the nerves of a groom on his wedding day. He stood by the altar that had been set up in the castle's largest feast hall, and somehow he managed to stand perfectly still—but only because his soldier's training kept him from showing any fear. Standing out in front of all of them, he could feel his stomach knotting with the pressure of it.

Thanos looked about while awaiting his bride. The feast hall swam in white silk and shone with diamonds, hardly a surface there that didn't glitter. Even the servants attending the nobles wore clothes that would have shamed most merchants. As for the nobles themselves, today they looked like something out of a bard's tale, dressed in silk and velvet, dripping with gold and silver.

To Thanos, it was far too much; yet he hadn't exactly been given a say in it. Delos's royals had gotten the wedding the king and queen decided they should have, and anything less than perfection would have disappointed his bride. He glanced over and saw them: King Claudius and Queen Athena, sitting together on thrones carved from ironwood and covered in gold leaf. They sat proudly, obviously delighted by his decision to accept their choice of bride.

The high priest, decked in a robe of gold reflecting the rays of the sun, stood beside him. He seemed like a kindly man, and Thanos, feeling more alone than ever, wanted to take him aside and ask him: *What do you do when you aren't sure that you belong somewhere?*

Yet he could not.

It wasn't just that Thanos was nervous about the wedding. It was so many other things as well. There was the fact that back on Haylon, the rebels there were relying on him to help them to free the Empire. That thought brought a flash of determination with it, because he *would* help them, whatever it took. Yet here he stood in this hall, surrounded by the enemy.

There was also the fact that Lucious was here, standing in the corner, dressed in royal purple and silver, smirking as he eyed the serving girls. Thanos had to fight to keep from walking over there and strangling him with his bare hands.

And then there was the thought that would not let him be:

Ceres.

1

That brought with it a spike of pain that felt, even now, as though it might burst through his chest. He could still barely believe that she was dead and gone, lost on a prison ship while he'd been on Haylon. Just the thought of that threatened to drag him back toward the darkness that had consumed him when he'd heard the news.

Stephania had pulled him out of that. She'd been the one shining point in it all, the only person in Delos who had brought him any happiness when he had wanted to end it all, when he could not envision a life without Ceres.

It was not that he did not love Stephania; he did. He had come to love her. It was, rather, that he could not let himself forget Ceres. It was as if the two loves still co-existed in his heart. He could not understand it all. Why had Ceres been meant to come into his life only to leave it? Why had Stephania been meant to come into his life at the moment she had? Had Ceres come to him to somehow prepare him to accept Stephania? Or had the two nothing to do with one another?

Music stirred. Thanos turned and his heart caught to see Stephania arrive to the strains of lyre music. His heart beat faster as she walked, all the nobles standing as she went, accompanied by handmaidens who threw rose petals and rang bells to drive away any lingering bad luck. Her dress was a pure, elegant white that made it look as though the whole room had been designed around it. She wore a diamond-studded caul over her golden hair, flowers worked into it with elaborate grace. The veil that covered her face shimmered with silver thread and tiny sapphires that mirrored the shade of the eyes beneath.

Thanos felt his fears melt away.

He watched as she approached, seeming to glide her way through the hall to the altar. She stood before him, and Thanos lifted the veil from her features.

He felt his breath catch. She was always lovely, but today she looked so perfect Thanos could barely believe that she was real. He stood staring at her for so long that he barely heard the priest begin the ceremony.

"The gods have given us many feasts and ceremonies in which to reflect on their glory," the high priest intoned. "Of these, marriage is the most sacred, for without it there would be no continuation of humankind. This marriage is an especially glorious one, between two of the great nobles of this realm. Yet it is also between a young man and a young woman who love one another deeply, and whose happiness should find a place in all our hearts."

He paused to let the words sink in.

"Prince Thanos, will you present your arm to be bound to this woman for all time? To love her and honor her until the gods take you from one another, and to see your families made one?"

He'd hesitated before, but now he didn't. He extended his arm toward the high priest, palm up. "I will."

"And Lady Stephania," the high priest continued, "will you present your arm to be bound to this man for all time? To love him and honor him until the gods take you from one another, and to see your families made one?"

Stephania's smile was the most beautiful thing Thanos had ever seen. She placed her hand in his. "I will."

The high priest wrapped a length of pure white cloth around and around their arms, the wrapping both traditional and elegant.

"Bound together in marriage, you are one flesh, one soul, one family," the high priest said. "May you be happy together always. You may kiss."

Thanos didn't need to be told. It was awkward, bound together like that, but that was always one of the minor amusements of a wedding feast, and they found a way. Thanos tasted Stephania's lips against his, melting into her, and for a moment at least, he could put aside all the other concerns in the world and just be there with her. Even thoughts of Ceres faded into the background, consumed in Stephania's touch.

Of course, Lucious would be the one to break the magic of the moment.

"Well, I'm glad that's done," he said over the silence of the crowd. "Can we start the party now? I need a drink!"

***

If the wedding ceremony had been opulent, the feast that followed was spectacular. So much so that Thanos found himself wondering about the cost of it. It looked as though half the profits from the latest raids had gone into it, with no expense spared. He knew that the king and queen were paying, as a way of showing how happy they were about the wedding, but how many families in the city could something like this have fed?

A glance around let him see tumblers and dancers, musicians and jugglers entertaining knots of nobles. Nobles danced together in swirling circles, while food was spread out in what seemed to Thanos like small mountains of pastries and sweetmeats, oysters and rich desserts.

3

There was wine, of course, enough that as the festivities continued, things grew wilder. The dancing sped up, with people spinning between partners almost faster than Thanos could follow. The king and queen had already retired, along with some of the older nobles, leaving the room. It was like a signal to the partygoers to put aside those inhibitions that remained.

Stephania was currently being whirled around in the traditional farewell dance, where the bride danced quickly between all the eligible young men in the room, before she would head back to Thanos's arms at the finish. Traditionally, it was a way for the bride to show how happy she was with her choice compared to all she was rejecting. More informally, it gave the young men a chance to show off to any of the other young noble women watching.

To Thanos's surprise, Lucious didn't join in the dance. He'd half expected the prince to do something foolish like trying to steal a kiss. Although, compared to the part where he'd tried to have Thanos killed, that would have been relatively innocuous.

Instead, the prince swaggered over while the dance was still in progress, pushing his way through the crowd with casual arrogance as he held a crystal goblet of the finest wine. Thanos looked at him and tried to find any similarity between them. They were both the king's offspring, but Thanos could never imagine being anything like Lucious.

"It's a beautiful wedding," Lucious said to him. "All the things I like best: good food, better wine, plenty of serving girls around for later."

"Watch yourself, Lucious," Thanos said.

"I have a better idea," Lucious countered. "Why don't we both watch that lovely bride of yours, spinning between so many men? Of course, with it being Stephania, we could have a small wager on which of them she's slept with."

Thanos's hands clenched into fists. "Are you just here to cause trouble? Because if so, you can get out."

Lucious's smile widened. "And how would that look, you trying to throw out the heir to the throne from your wedding? That wouldn't go well."

"Not for you."

"Remember your place, Thanos," Lucious snapped back.

"Oh, I know my place," Thanos said in a dangerous voice. "We both do, don't we?"

That got a faint flicker of reaction from Lucious. Even if Thanos hadn't known it, it would have been confirmation: Lucious knew about the circumstances of Thanos's birth. He knew they were half-brothers.

"Curse you and your marriage," Lucious said.

"You're just jealous," Thanos countered. "I know you wanted Stephania for yourself, and now I'm the one marrying her. I'm the one who didn't run away in the Stade. I'm the one who actually fought on Haylon. We both know what else I am. So what's left for you, Lucious? You're just a thug the people of Delos need protecting from."

Thanos heard the crack as Lucious's hand tightened around his crystal goblet, squeezing until it shattered.

"You like to protect the lesser orders, don't you?" Lucious said. "Well, think about this: while you've been planning a wedding, I've been crushing villages. I will continue to do it. In fact, while you're still in your marriage bed tomorrow morning, I'll be riding out to teach another bunch of peasants a lesson. And there is *nothing* you can do about it, whoever you think you are."

Thanos wanted to hit Lucious then. He wanted to hit him and keep hitting him until there was nothing left but a bloody smear on the marble floor. The only thing that stopped him was the touch of Stephania's hand on his arm, approaching as her dance ended.

"Oh, Lucious, you've spilled your wine," she said with a smile that Thanos wished he could match. "That won't do at all. Allow one of my attendants to fetch you more."

"I'll get my own," Lucious replied with obvious bad grace. "They got me this one, and look what happened to it."

He stalked off, and only the pull of Stephania's hand on his arm stopped Thanos from following.

"Leave it," Stephania said. "I told you there are better ways, and there are. Trust me."

"He can't just get away with all he's done," Thanos insisted.

"He won't. Look at it this way though," she said. "Who would you rather spend the evening with? Lucious, or me?"

That brought a smile to Thanos's lips. "You. Definitely you."

Stephania kissed him. "Good answer."

Thanos felt her hand slip into his, pulling him in the direction of the doors. The other nobles there let them pass, with occasional laughs about what would happen next. Thanos followed as Stephania led the way to Thanos's rooms, pushing the door open and heading in the direction of the bed chamber. There, she turned to him, throwing her arms around his neck and kissing him deeply.

"You don't have any regrets?" Stephania asked, as she stepped back from him. "You're happy you married me?"

"I'm very happy," Thanos assured her. "What about you?"

"It's all I ever wanted," Stephania said. "And you know what I want now?"

"What?"

Thanos saw her reach up, and her dress fell from her in waves. "You."

***

Thanos woke to the first rays of sunlight spilling through the windows. Beside him, he could feel the warm pressure of Stephania's presence, one of her arms thrown across him as she slept curled against him. Thanos smiled at the love welling up inside him. He was happier right now than he had been in a long time.

If he hadn't heard the clink of harness and the whinnying of horses, he might have curled up against Stephania again and gone back to sleep, or woken her with a kiss. As it was, he rose, heading over to the window.

He was just in time to see Lucious leaving the castle, riding at the head of a group of soldiers, pennants flying in the wind as if he were some knight-errant on a quest rather than a butcher preparing to attack a defenseless village. Thanos looked out at him, then over at where Stephania was still sleeping.

Silently, he started to dress.

He couldn't stand by. He couldn't, not even for Stephania. She'd talked about better ways of dealing with Lucious, but what did they involve? Politeness and offering him wine? No, Lucious had to be stopped, right now, and there was only one way to do it.

Quietly, taking care not to wake Stephania, Thanos slipped from the room. Once he was clear, he ran for the stables, shouting for a servant to bring him his armor.

It was time for justice.

CHAPTER TWO

Berin could feel the excitement, the nervous energy palpable in the air the moment he stepped into the tunnels. He weaved his way underground, following Anka, Sartes by his side, passing guards who nodded with respect, rebels who hurried every which way. He walked through the Watcher's Gate and felt the turn the Rebellion had taken.

Now, it seemed, they had a chance.

"This way," Anka said, waving to a lookout. "The others await us."

They walked down corridors of bare stone that looked as if they had stood forever. The Ruins of Delos, deep underground. Berin ran his hand along the smooth stone, admiring them as only a smith could, and marveled at how long these had stood, at who had built them. Maybe they even dated back to the days when the Ancient Ones had walked, long before anyone could remember.

And that made him think, with a pang, of the daughter he had lost.

Ceres.

Berin was yanked from that thought by the clang of hammers on metal, by the sudden heat of forge fires as they passed an opening. He saw a dozen men toiling away as they tried to produce breastplates and short swords. It reminded him of his old smithy, and brought back memories of the days when his family hadn't been torn apart.

Sartes seemed to be staring, too.

"Are you all right?" Berin asked.

He nodded.

"I miss her too," Berin replied, putting a hand on his shoulder, knowing he was thinking of Ceres, who always lingered by the forge.

"We all do," Anka chimed in.

For a moment the three of them stood there, and Berin knew that they all understood how much Ceres had meant to them.

He heard Anka sigh.

"All we can do is keep fighting," she added, "and keep forging weapons. We need you, Berin."

He tried to focus.

"Are they doing everything I instructed?" he asked. "Are they heating the metal enough before quenching? It won't harden otherwise."

7

Anka smiled.

"Check for yourself after the meeting."

Berin nodded. At least in some small way he could be useful.

***

Sartes walked by his father's side, following Anka as they continued past the forge and deeper through the tunnels. There were more people in them than he could have believed. Men and women were gathering supplies, practicing with weapons, pacing the halls. Sartes recognized several of them as former conscripts, freed from the army's clutches.

They finally came upon a cavernous space, set with stone plinths that might once have held statues. By the light of flickering candles, Sartes could see the leaders of the rebellion, awaiting them. Hannah, who had argued against the attack, now looked as happy as if she'd proposed it. Oreth, one of Anka's main deputies now, leaned his slender frame against the wall, smiling to himself. Sartes spotted the larger bulk of the former wharf hand Edrin on the edge of the candlelight, while Yeralt's jewels shone in it, the merchant's son looking almost out of place among the rest as they laughed and joked among themselves.

They fell silent as the three of them approached, and Sartes could see the difference now. Before, they'd listened to Anka almost grudgingly. Now, after the ambush, there was respect there as she walked forward. She even looked more like a leader to Sartes, walking straighter, appearing more confident.

"Anka, Anka, Anka!" Oreth began, and soon the others took up the chant, as the rebels had after the battle.

Sartes joined in, hearing the rebel leader's name echo around the space. He only stopped when Anka gestured for silence.

"We did well," Anka said, with a smile of her own. It was one of the first Sartes had seen since the battle. She'd been too busy trying to arrange to get their casualties away from the burial ground safely. She had a talent for seeing to the details of things that had blossomed in the rebellion.

"*Well?*" Edrin asked. "We smashed them."

Sartes heard the thud of the man's fist against his palm as he emphasized the point.

"We destroyed them," Yeralt agreed, "thanks to your leadership."

8

Anka shook her head. "We beat them together. We beat them because we all did our parts. And because Sartes brought us the plans."

Sartes found himself pushed forward by his father. He hadn't been expecting this.

"Anka is right," Oreth said. "We owe Sartes our thanks. He brought us the plans, and he was the one to persuade the conscripts not to fight. The rebellion has more members, thanks to him."

"Half-trained conscripts though," Hannah said. "Not real soldiers."

Sartes looked around at her. She'd been quick to argue against him taking part at all. He didn't like her, but it wasn't about that in the rebellion. They were all a part of something bigger than themselves.

"We beat them," Anka said. "We won a battle, but that isn't the same thing as smashing the Empire. We still have a lot ahead of us."

"And they still have a lot of soldiers," Yeralt said. "A long war against them could prove costly for all of us."

"You're counting the cost now?" Oreth countered. "This isn't some business investment, where you want to see the balance sheets before you get involved."

Sartes could hear the annoyance there. When he'd first come to the rebels, he'd expected them to be some big, unified thing, thinking of nothing but the need to defeat the Empire. He'd found out that in a lot of ways they were just people, all with their own hopes and dreams, wishes and wants. It only made it more impressive that Anka had found ways to hold them together after Rexus died.

"It's the biggest investment there is," Yeralt said. "We put in all we have. We risk our lives in the hope that things will get better. I'm in as much danger as the rest of you if we fail."

"We won't fail," Edrin said. "We beat them once. We'll beat them again. We know where they're going to attack and when. We can be waiting for them every time."

"We can do more than that," Hannah said. "We've shown people that we can beat them, so why not go out and take things back from them?"

"What did you have in mind?" Anka asked. Sartes could see that she was considering it.

"We take villages back one by one," Hannah said. "We get rid of the Empire's soldiers in them before Lucious can get close. We show the people there what's possible, and he'll get a nasty surprise when they rise up against him."

"And when Lucious and his men kill them for rising up?" Oreth demanded. "What then?"

"Then it just shows how evil he is," Hannah insisted.

"Or people see that we can't protect them."

Sartes looked around, surprised they were taking the idea seriously.

"We could leave people in the villages so that they don't fall," Yeralt suggested. "We have the conscripts with us now."

"They won't stand against the army for long if it comes," Oreth shot back. "They'd die along with the villagers."

Sartes knew he was right. The conscripts hadn't had the training that the toughest soldiers in the army had. Worse, they'd suffered so much at the hands of the army that most of them would probably be terrified.

He saw Anka gesture for silence. This time, it took a little longer in coming.

"Oreth has a point," she said.

"Of course you'd agree with *him*," Hannah shot back.

"I'm agreeing because he's right," Anka said. "We can't just go into villages, declare them free, and hope for the best. Even with the conscripts, we don't have enough fighters. If we join together in one place, we give the Empire an opportunity to crush us. If we go after every village, they'll pick us apart piecemeal."

"If enough villages can be persuaded to rise up, and I persuade my father to hire mercenaries..." Yeralt suggested. Sartes noted he didn't finish the thought. The merchant's son didn't have an answer, not really.

"Then what?" Anka asked. "We'll have the numbers? If it were that simple, we would have overthrown the Empire years ago."

"We have better weapons now thanks to Berin," Edrin pointed out. "We know their plans thanks to Sartes. We have the advantage! Tell her, Berin. Tell her about the blades you've made."

Sartes looked around to his father, who shrugged.

"It's true I've made good swords, and the others here have made plenty of passable ones. It's true that some of you will have armor now, rather than being cut down. But I'll tell you this: it's about more than the sword. It's about the hand that wields it. An army is like a blade. You can make it as big as you want, but without a core of good steel, it will break the first time you test it."

Maybe if the others had spent more time making weapons, they would have understood how seriously his father meant his words. As it was, Sartes could see they weren't convinced.

"What else can we do?" Edrin asked. "We're not just going to throw away our advantage by sitting back and waiting. I say that we start making a list of villages to free. Unless you have a better idea, Anka?"

"I do," Sartes said.

His voice was quieter than he intended. He stepped forward, his heart pounding, surprised that he had spoken. He was all too aware that he was far younger than anyone else there. He'd played his part in the battle, he'd even killed a man, but there was still a part of him that felt as though he shouldn't be speaking there.

"So it's settled," Hannah started to say. "We—"

"I said I have a better idea," Sartes said, and this time, his voice carried.

The others looked over at him.

"Let my son speak," his father said. "You've said yourselves that he helped to hand one victory to you. Maybe he can keep you from dying now."

"What's your idea, Sartes?" Anka asked.

They were all looking at him. Sartes forced himself to raise his voice, thinking about how Ceres would have spoken, but also about the confidence Anka had shown before.

"We can't go to the villages," Sartes said. "It's what they want us to do. And we can't just rely on the maps I brought, because even if they haven't realized that we know their movements, they will soon. They're trying to goad us out into the open."

"We know all this," Yeralt said. "I thought you said you had a plan."

Sartes didn't back down.

"What if there were a way to hit the Empire where they don't expect it and gain tough fighters into the bargain? What if we could make people rise up with a symbolic victory that would be bigger than protecting a village?"

"What did you have in mind?" Anka asked.

"We free the combatlords in the Stade," Sartes said.

A long, stunned silence followed, as the others stared at him. He could see the doubt in their faces, and Sartes knew he had to keep going.

"Think about it," he said. "Almost all combatlords are slaves. The nobles throw them in to die like toys. Most of them would be

11

grateful for the chance to get away, and they can fight better than any soldiers."

"It's insane," Hannah said. "Attacking the heart of the city like that. There would be guards everywhere."

"I like it," Anka said.

The others looked at her, and Sartes felt a rush of gratitude for her support.

"They wouldn't expect it," she added.

Another silence fell over the room.

"We wouldn't need mercenaries," Yeralt finally chimed in, rubbing his chin.

"People would rise up," Edrin added.

"We'd have to do it when the Killings were on," Oreth pointed out. "That way, all the combatlords would be in one place, and there would be people there to see it happen."

"There won't be more Killings before the Blood Moon festival," his father said. "That's six weeks. In six weeks, I can make a lot of weapons."

This time, Hannah fell silent, perhaps sensing the tide turn.

"So we're agreed?" Anka asked. "We'll free the combatlords during the Blood Moon festival?"

One by one, Sartes saw the others nod. Even Hannah did, eventually. He felt his father's hand on his shoulder. He saw the approval in his eyes, and it meant the world to him.

He only prayed that his plan would not get them all killed.

CHAPTER THREE

Ceres dreamed, and in her dreams, she saw armies clashing. She saw herself fighting at their head, dressed in armor that shone in the sun. She saw herself leading a vast nation, fighting a war that would determine the very fate of mankind.

Yet in it all, she also saw herself squinting, searching for her mother. She reached for a sword, and looked down to see it was not yet there.

Ceres woke with a start. It was night, and the sea before her, lit by the moonlight, was endless. As she bobbed in her small ship, she saw no sign of land. Only the stars convinced her that she was still keeping her small craft on the right course.

Familiar constellations shone overhead. There was the Dragon's Tail, low in the sky beneath the moon. There was the Ancient's Eye, formed around one of the brightest stars in the stretch of blackness. The ship that the forest folk had half built, half grown seemed never to deviate from the route Ceres had picked out, even when she had to rest or eat.

Off the starboard side of the boat, Ceres saw lights in the water. Luminous jellyfish floated past like underwater clouds. Ceres saw the faster figure of some dart-like fish slipping through the shoal, snapping up jellyfish with every pass and hurrying through before the tendrils of the others could touch it. Ceres watched until they disappeared down into the depths.

She ate a piece of the sweet, succulent fruit the islanders had stocked her boat with. When she'd set off it had seemed as though there was enough to last for weeks. Now, it didn't seem like quite so much. She found herself thinking of the leader of the forest folk, so handsome in a strange, asymmetrical way, with his curse lending him patches where his skin was mossy green or roughened like bark. Would he be back on the island, playing his strange music and thinking of her?

Around Ceres, mist started to rise up from the water, thickening and reflecting fragments of the moonlight even as it blocked out her view of the night sky above. It swirled and shifted around the boat, tendrils of fog reaching out like fingers. Thoughts of Eoin seemed to lead inexorably to thoughts of Thanos. Thanos, who'd been killed on the shores of Haylon before Ceres could tell him that she hadn't meant any of the harsh things she'd said when he left. There in the boat alone, Ceres couldn't get away from just how much she missed him. The love she'd felt for him felt like a thread pulling her back toward Delos, even though Thanos was no longer there.

Thinking of Thanos hurt. The memory felt like an open wound that might never close. There were so many things she needed to do, but none of them would bring him back. There were so many things she would have said if he were there, but he wasn't. There was only the emptiness of the mist.

The mist continued to coil around the boat, and now Ceres could see shards of rock sticking up out of the water. Some were razor-edged black basalt, but others were in rainbow colors, seeming like giant precious stones set in the roiling blue of the ocean. Some had markings on them that swirled and spiraled, and Ceres wasn't sure whether they were natural, or if some long distant hand had carved them.

Did her mother lie somewhere beyond them?

The thought brought a thrill of excitement in Ceres, rising up through her like the mist that swirled around the boat. She was going to see her mother. Her real mother, not the one who had always hated her, and who had sold her to slavers at the first opportunity. Ceres didn't know what this woman would be like, but just the opportunity to find out filled her with excitement as she guided the small boat along past the rocks.

Strong currents pulled at her boat, threatening to pull the rudder from her hand. If she hadn't had the strength that came from the power within her, Ceres doubted that she would have been able to hold on. She pulled the rudder to the side, and her small boat responded with an almost living grace, slipping past one of the rocks almost close enough to touch it.

She sailed on through the rocks, and with every one she passed, she found herself thinking about how much closer she was getting to her mother. What kind of woman would she be? In her visions, she'd been indistinct, but Ceres could imagine, and hope. Maybe she would be kind, and gentle, and loving; all the things she'd never had from her supposed mother back in Delos.

What would her mother think of her? That thought caught at Ceres as she guided the boat onward through the mist. She didn't know what was ahead. Maybe her mother would look at her and see someone who hadn't been able to succeed in the Stade, who had been nothing more than a slave in the Empire, who had lost the person she loved most. What if her mother rejected her? What if she were harsh, or cruel, or unforgiving?

Or maybe, just maybe, she would be proud.

Ceres came out of the mist so suddenly that it might have been a curtain lifting, and now the sea was flat, free of the tooth-like rocks that had jutted from it before. Instantly, she could see that there was something different. The light of the moon seemed brighter somehow, and around it, nebulae spun in stains of color on the night. Even the stars seemed changed, so that now, Ceres couldn't pick out the familiar constellations there had been before. A comet streaked its way across the horizon, fiery red mixed with yellows and other colors that had no equivalent in the world below.

Stranger than that, Ceres felt the power within her pulse, as though responding to this place. It seemed to stretch within her, opening out and allowing her to experience this new place in a hundred ways she'd never thought of before.

Ceres saw a shape rise from the water, a long, serpentine neck rising up before plunging back beneath the waves with a splash of spray. The creature rose again briefly, and Ceres had the impression of something huge swimming past in the water before it was gone. What looked like birds flitted through the moonlight, and it was only as they got closer that Ceres saw that they were silvery moths, larger than her head.

Her eyes suddenly growing heavy with sleep, Ceres lashed the tiller in place, lay down, and let sleep overcome her.

***

Ceres woke to the shriek of birds. She blinked in the sunlight as she sat up, and saw that they weren't birds after all. Two creatures with the bodies of great cats wheeled overhead on eagle-like wings, raptor beaks wide as they called. They showed no signs of coming closer though, merely circling the boat before flying off into the distance.

Ceres watched them, and because she was watching them, she saw the tiny speck of an island they were heading for on the horizon. As quickly as she could, Ceres raised the small sail again, trying to catch the wind that rushed past her to push herself toward the island.

The speck grew larger, and what looked like more rocks rose out of the ocean as Ceres got closer, but these weren't the same as the ones that had been there in the mist. These were square-edged, built things, crafted in rainbow marble. Some of them looked like the spires of great buildings, long sunk beneath the waves.

Half an arch stuck out, so huge that Ceres couldn't imagine what might have passed beneath it. She looked down over the side of the boat, and the water was so clear that she could make out the sea bed below. It wasn't far to the bottom, and Ceres could see the wreckage of long past buildings down there. It was close enough that Ceres could have swum down to them just by holding her breath. She didn't, though, both because of the things she'd already seen in the water and because of what lay ahead.

This was it. The island where she would get the answers she needed. Where she would learn about her power.

Where she would, finally, meet her mother.

CHAPTER FOUR

Lucious swung his blade overhand, exulting in the way it glinted in the dawn light, in the instant before he cut down the old man who had dared to get in his way. Around him, more commoners fell at the hands of his men: the ones who dared to resist, and any stupid enough to simply be in the wrong place at the wrong time.

He smiled as the screams echoed around him. He liked it when the peasants tried to fight, because it just gave his men an excuse to show them how weak they really were compared to their betters. How many had he killed now in raids like this? He hadn't bothered to keep count. Why should he save the least speck of attention for their kind?

Lucious looked around as peasants started to run, and gestured to a few of his men. They set off after them. Running was almost better than fighting, because there was a challenge to hunting them like the prey they were.

"Your horse, your highness?" one of the men asked, leading Lucious's stallion.

Lucious shook his head. "My bow, I think."

The man nodded and passed Lucious an elegant recurve bow of white ash, mixed with horn and set with silver. He nocked an arrow, drew back the string, and let it fly. Away in the distance, one of the running peasants went down.

There were no more to fight, but that didn't mean they were done here. Not by a long way. Hiding peasants, he'd found, could be as amusing as running or fighting ones in their way. There were so many different ways to torture the ones who looked as though they had gold, and so many ways to execute the ones who might have rebel sympathies. The burning wheel, the gibbet, the noose... what would it be today?

Lucious gestured to a couple of his men to start kicking open doors. Occasionally, he liked to burn out those who hid, but houses were more valuable than peasants. A woman came running out, and Lucious caught her, throwing her casually in the direction of one of the slavers who had taken to following him around like gulls after a fishing vessel.

He stalked into the village's temple. The priest was already on the ground, holding a broken nose, while Lucious's men gathered gold and silver ornaments into a sack. A woman in the robes of a priestess stood to confront him. Lucious noted a flicker of blonde hair straying from under her cowl, a certain fine-featured resemblance that made him pause.

"You can't do this," the woman insisted. "We are a temple!"

Lucious grabbed her, pulling away the hood of her robes to look at her. She wasn't the double of Stephania—no lower-born woman could manage that—but she was close enough to be worth keeping for a while. At least until he got bored.

"I have been sent by your king," Lucious said. "Do *not* try to tell me what I cannot do!"

Too many people had tried that in his life. They'd tried to put limits on him, when he was the one person in the Empire on whom there should be no limits. His parents tried, but he would be king one day. He *would* be king, whatever he'd found in the library when old Cosmas thought he was too stupid to understand it. Thanos would learn his place.

Lucious's hand tightened in the hair of the priestess. Stephania would learn her place as well. How dare she marry Thanos like that, as if he were the prince to be desired? No, Lucious would find a way to make that right. He would split Thanos and Stephania as easily as he split open the heads of those who came at him. He would claim Stephania in marriage, both because she was Thanos's and because she would make the perfect ornament for someone of his rank. He would enjoy that, and until then, the priestess he'd grabbed would make a suitable substitute.

He tossed her to one of his men to watch, and set out to see what other amusements he could find in the village. As he got outside, he saw two of his men tying one of the villagers who'd run to a tree, arms spread wide.

"Why have you let this one live?" Lucious demanded.

One of them smiled. "Tor here was telling me about something the northerners do. They call it the Blood Eagle."

Lucious liked the sound of that. He was about to ask what it involved when he heard the shout of one of the lookouts, there to watch for rebels. Lucious looked around, but instead of an approaching horde of common scum, he saw a single figure riding on a mount easily the size of his own. Lucious recognized the armor instantly.

"Thanos," he said. He snapped his fingers. "Well, it looks as though today is about to get more interesting than I thought. Bring me my bow again."

***

18

Thanos spurred his horse forward as he saw Lucious and what his half-brother was doing. Any lingering doubts he'd had about leaving Stephania behind burned away in the heat of his anger as he saw the dead peasants, the slavers, the man tied to the tree.

He saw Lucious step out and raise a bow. For a moment, Thanos couldn't believe that he would do it, but why not? Lucious had tried to kill him before.

He saw the arrow fly out from the bow and raised his shield just in time. The head struck the metal facing of his shield before clattering off. A second arrow followed, and this time it punched through, stopping only inches from Thanos's face.

Thanos forced his horse to a charge as a third arrow whizzed past him. He saw Lucious and his men diving out of the way as he careened through the spot where they'd been standing. He wheeled and drew his sword, just as Lucious regained his feet.

"Thanos, so fast. Anyone would think you were eager to see me."

Thanos leveled his sword at Lucious's heart. "This stops now, Lucious. I won't let you kill any more of our people."

"Our people?" Lucious countered. "They are *my* people, Thanos. Mine to do what I wish with. Allow me to demonstrate."

Thanos saw him draw his sword and start toward the man tied to the tree. Thanos realized what his half-brother was going to do and set his horse in motion once more.

"Stop him," Lucious commanded.

His men leapt to obey. One stepped toward Thanos, jabbing a spear up toward his face. Thanos deflected it with his shield, hacking the head from the weapon with his blade and then kicking out to send the man sprawling. He stabbed down as another ran at him, thrusting down through the shoulder of the man's mail and drawing his blade out again.

He forced himself forward, through the press of opponents. Lucious was still advancing on the victim he'd chosen. Thanos swung his sword down at one of Lucious's thugs and hurried forward as Lucious drew his own blade back. Thanos barely managed to interject his shield as the blow came in a ring of metal on metal.

Lucious grabbed his shield.

"You're predictable, Thanos," he said. "Compassion was always your weakness."

He pulled, hard enough that Thanos found himself yanked from the saddle. He rolled in time to avoid a sword blow, and pulled his arm free from the straps of his shield. He took a two-handed grip on his sword as Lucious's men closed in again. He saw his horse run clear, but that meant that now he didn't have the advantage of height.

"Kill him," Lucious said. "We'll blame it on the rebels."

"You're good at trying that, aren't you?" Thanos shot back. "It's a pity you aren't any good at finishing the job."

One of Lucious's men rushed him then, swinging a spiked mace. Thanos stepped inside the arc of the blow, cutting diagonally, then spinning away with his sword extended to keep the others at bay.

They came in quickly then, as if knowing that none of them could hope to defeat Thanos one on one. Thanos gave ground, putting his back against the wall of the nearest house so that his opponents couldn't surround him. There were three men near him now, one with an axe, one with a short sword, and one with a curved blade like a sickle.

Thanos kept his sword close, watching them, not wanting to give any of the mercenaries a chance to tangle the blade long enough for the others to slip in.

The one on Thanos's right tried a thrust with his short sword. Thanos partly parried it, feeling it clatter off his armor. Some instinct made him spin and drop, just in time for the left-hand man's axe to pass overhead. Thanos slashed at ankle height to bring the thug down, then reversed his blade and thrust backward, hearing a cry as the first man ran in.

The one with the curved blade attacked more cautiously.

"Attack him! Kill him!" Lucious demanded, obviously impatient. "Oh, I'll do it myself!"

Thanos parried as the prince joined the fight. He doubted that Lucious would have done it if there hadn't been another man there to help him, and maybe there would be more on the way. Really, all Lucious had to do was delay things, and Thanos might find himself overwhelmed by sheer numbers.

So Thanos didn't wait. Instead, he attacked. He threw blow after blow, alternating between Lucious and the thug Lucious had brought with him, building the rhythm of it. Then, suddenly, he paused. The sickle wielder parried empty air. Thanos cut into the gap, and the man's head went flying.

He was on Lucious in an instant, binding blade to blade. Lucious kicked out at him, but Thanos swayed aside from the blow, reaching over the guard of Lucious's sword to get one hand onto the pommel. Thanos yanked upward and wrenched the blade from Lucious's hands, then struck sideways. His blade clanged from

Lucious's breastplate. Lucious drew a dagger and Thanos changed his grip on his blade, swinging low with the hilt end so that the cross-guard hooked around Lucious's knee.

He pulled and Lucious went down. Thanos kicked the dagger from his hand with crunching force.

"Tell me again how compassion is my weakness," Thanos said, lifting the point of his sword over Lucious's throat.

"You wouldn't," Lucious said. "You're just trying to frighten me."

"Frighten you?" Thanos said. "If I thought frightening you would work, I'd have scared you half to death years ago. No, I'm going to end this."

"End it?" Lucious said. "This doesn't *end*, Thanos. Not until I've *won*."

"You'd be waiting a long time for that," Thanos assured him.

He raised the sword. He had to do this. Lucious had to be stopped.

"Thanos!"

Thanos looked over at the sound of Stephania's voice. To his astonishment, he saw her approaching, riding alone at a full gallop. She wore a riding outfit that was a long way from her usual elegant dresses, and from the disheveled state of it, it looked as though she'd thrown it on in a hurry.

"Thanos, don't!" she cried as she got closer.

Thanos gripped his sword tighter. "After all he's done, do you think he doesn't deserve it?"

"It's not about what he deserves," Stephania said, dismounting as she got closer. "It's about what you deserve. If you kill him, they'll kill you for it. That's how it works, and I will *not* lose you like that."

"Listen to her, Thanos," Lucious said from the ground.

"Be quiet," Stephania snapped. "Or do you want to goad him into killing you?"

"He has to be stopped," Thanos said.

"Not like this," Stephania insisted. Thanos felt her hand on his arm, pushing the sword away. "Not in a way that gets you killed. You swore you would be mine for the rest of our lives. Did you really mean for it to be so short?"

"Stephania—" Thanos began, but she didn't let him finish.

"And what about me?" she asked. "How much danger will I be in if my husband kills the heir to the throne? No, Thanos. Stop this. Do it for me."

If anyone else had asked, Thanos might still have gone through with it. There was too much at stake. But he couldn't risk Stephania. He thrust down into the dirt, missing Lucious's head by an inch. Lucious was already rolling away, running for a horse.

"You'll regret this!" Lucious called back. "I promise you'll regret this!"

CHAPTER FIVE

Thanos saw the guards awaiting him on the long run into the city gates, as he and Stephania returned home. He raised his chin and kept on riding. He had expected this. And he wouldn't run from it.

Stephania obviously saw them too. Thanos saw her stiffen in the saddle, going from relaxed to prim and formal in an instant. It was as though a mask had slid down in front of her features, and Thanos found himself reaching out automatically to slide a hand over hers as she held the reins.

The guards crossed their halberds to bar the way as they approached, and Thanos drew his horse to a halt. He kept it between Stephania and the guards, just in case Lucious had somehow bribed men to attack him. He saw an officer step out from the knot of guards and salute.

"Prince Thanos, welcome back to Delos. My men and I have been instructed to escort you to see the king."

"And if my husband does not wish to travel with you?" Stephania asked, in a tone that could have commanded the whole Empire.

"Forgive me, my lady," the officer said, "but the king has given us clear orders."

Thanos raised a hand before Stephania could argue.

"I understand," he said. "I'll go with you."

The guards led the way, and to their credit, they managed to make it look like the escort they claimed it was. They led the way through Delos, and Thanos noted that the route they picked was one through the most beautiful parts of the city, sticking to the tree-lined avenues that held noble houses, avoiding the worst parts even when they formed a more direct route. Perhaps they were simply trying to stick to the safer areas. Perhaps, though, they thought that nobles like Thanos and Stephania wouldn't want to see the misery elsewhere.

Soon, the walls of the castle towered above. The guards led the way through its gates, and grooms took their horses. The walk through the castle felt more confined, with so many guards surrounding them in the narrow spaces of the castle corridors. Stephania took Thanos's hand, and he squeezed it gently in reassurance.

When they reached the royal apartments, members of the royal bodyguard blocked the way at the door.

"The king wishes to speak to Prince Thanos alone," one said.

"I am his wife," Stephania said in a tone so cold Thanos suspected most people would have stepped aside instantly.

It didn't seem to affect the royal bodyguard at all. "Nevertheless."

"It will be all right," Thanos said.

When he stepped inside, the king was waiting for him. King Claudius stood, leaning on a sword whose hilt formed the tentacles of a twisting kraken. It came almost to the level of his chest, and Thanos had no doubt that the edge would be razor sharp. Thanos heard the click of the door shutting behind him.

"Lucious told me what you did," the king said.

"I'm sure he came running straight to you," Thanos replied. "Did he also tell you what he was doing at the time?"

"He was doing what he was commanded to," the king snapped, "in order to deal with the rebellion. Yet you went out and attacked him. You killed his men. He says you defeated him through trickery, and would have killed him too if Stephania hadn't intervened."

"How does butchering villagers stop the rebellion?" Thanos countered.

"You're more interested in peasants than in your own actions," King Claudius said. He lifted the sword he held as though weighing it. "It is treason to attack the king's son."

"*I* am the king's son," Thanos reminded him. "You didn't execute Lucious when he tried to have me killed."

"Your birth is the only reason you are still alive," King Claudius replied. "You are my son, but so is Lucious. You do *not* get to threaten him."

Anger rose up in Thanos then. "I don't get anything that I can see. Not even the acknowledgment of who I am."

There were statues in one corner of the room, depicting famous ancestors of the royal line. They were out of the way, almost hidden away, as if the king didn't want to be reminded of them. Even so, Thanos pointed to them.

"Lucious can look at those and claim authority going back to the days when the Empire first rose," he said. "He can claim the rights of all those who gained the throne when the Ancient Ones left Delos. What do I have? Vague rumors about my birth? Half-remembered images of parents that I'm not even sure are real?"

King Claudius strode to the spot in his rooms where his great chair sat. He sat upon it, cradling the sword he held across his knees.

24

"You have an honored place at court," he said.

"An honored place at court?" Thanos replied. "I have a place as a spare prince no one wants. Lucious might have tried to have me killed on Haylon, but you were the one who sent me there."

"Rebellion must be crushed, wherever it is found," the king countered. Thanos saw him run his thumb along the edge of the sword he held. "You had to learn that."

"Oh, I've learned," Thanos said, moving across to stand in front of his father. "I've learned that you would rather be rid of me than acknowledge me. I am your eldest son. By the laws of the kingdom, I ought to be your heir. The eldest son has been the heir since the first days of Delos."

"The eldest surviving son," the king said quietly. "You think you would have lived if people knew?"

"Don't pretend you were protecting me," Thanos replied. "You were protecting yourself."

"Better than spending my time fighting on behalf of people who don't even deserve it," the king said. "Do you know how it looks when you go around protecting peasants who should know their place?"

"It looks as though someone cares about them!" Thanos shouted. He couldn't keep from raising his voice then, because it seemed like the only way to get through to his father. Maybe if he could make him understand, then the Empire might finally change for the better. "It looks as though their rulers aren't enemies out to kill them, but people to be respected. It looks as though their lives mean something to us, rather than just being something for us to throw aside while we have glittering parties!"

The king was silent for a long time after that. Thanos could see the fury in his eyes. That was fine. It matched the anger Thanos felt almost perfectly.

"Kneel," King Claudius said at last.

Thanos hesitated, only for a second, but it was apparently enough.

"Kneel!" the king bellowed. "Or do you wish me to have you made to? I am still the king here!"

Thanos knelt on the hard stone of the floor before the king's chair. He saw the king raise the sword he held with difficulty, as though it had been a long time since he'd done it.

Thanos's thoughts went to the sword at his own side. He had no doubt that if it came to a battle between him and the king, he would be the winner. He was younger, stronger, and had trained with the best the Stade had to offer. But that would mean killing his father. More than that, it really would be treason.

"I have learned many things in my life," the king said, and the sword was still poised there. "When I was your age, I was like you. I was young, I was strong. I fought, and I fought well. I killed men in battle, and in duels in the Stade. I tried to fight for everything I believed to be right."

"What happened to you?" Thanos asked.

The king's lip curled into a sneer. "I learned better. I learned that if you give them a chance, people do not come together to lift you up. Instead, they try to tear you down. I have tried showing compassion, and the truth is that it is nothing more than foolishness. If a man stands against you, then you destroy him, because if you do not, he will destroy you."

"Or you make him your friend," Thanos said, "and he helps you to make things better."

"Friends?" King Claudius raised his sword another inch. "Powerful men have no friends. They have allies, servants, and hangers-on, but do not think for a moment that they will not turn on you. A sensible man keeps them in their place, or he watches them rise up against him."

"The people deserve better than that," Thanos insisted.

"You think people get what they deserve?" King Claudius bellowed. "They get what they take! You're talking as if you think the people are our equals. They aren't. We are raised from birth to rule them. We are more educated, stronger, better in every way. You want to put pig farmers in castles beside you, when I want to show them that they belong in their sty. Lucious understands."

"Lucious only understands cruelty," Thanos said.

"And cruelty is what it takes to rule!"

Thanos saw the king swing the sword then. Perhaps he could have ducked. Perhaps he could even have made a move for his own blade. Instead, he knelt there and watched as the sword swept down toward his throat, tracking the arc of the steel in the sunlight.

It stopped short of cutting his throat, but not by much. Thanos felt the sting as the edge touched his flesh, but he didn't react, no matter how much he wanted to.

"You didn't flinch," King Claudius said. "You barely even blinked. Lucious would have. Would probably have begged for his life. That is his weakness. But Lucious has the strength to do what is needed to hold our rule in place. *That* is why he is my heir. Until you can carve this weakness from your heart, I will not acknowledge you. I will not call you mine. And if you attack my acknowledged son again, I will have your head for it. Do you understand?"

Thanos stood. He'd had enough of kneeling to this man. "I understand, Father. I understand you perfectly."

He turned and walked for the doors, not waiting for permission to do it. What could his father do? It would look weak to call him back. Thanos stepped out, and Stephania was waiting for him. She looked as though she'd maintained her image of composure for the benefit of the bodyguards there, but the moment Thanos came out, she hurried forward to him.

"Are you all right?" Stephania asked, raising a hand to his cheek. It dropped lower, and Thanos saw it come away with blood on it. "Thanos, you're bleeding!"

"It's only a scratch," Thanos assured her. "I probably have worse from the fight earlier."

"What happened in there?" she demanded.

Thanos forced a smile, but it came out tighter than he intended. "His majesty chose to remind me that prince or not, I am not worth as much to him as Lucious."

Stephania put her hands on his shoulders. "I told you, Thanos. It was the wrong thing to do. You can't put yourself at risk like that. You have to promise me that you will trust me, and never do anything so foolish again. Promise me."

He nodded.

"For you, my love, I promise."

He meant it, too. Going and fighting Lucious in the open like that wasn't the right strategy, because it didn't achieve enough. Lucious wasn't the problem. The whole Empire was the problem. He'd briefly thought that he might be able to persuade the king to change things, but the truth was that his father didn't *want* things to change.

No, the only thing to do now was to find ways to help the rebellion. Not just the rebels on Haylon, but all of them. Alone, Thanos couldn't accomplish much, but together, they might just bring down the Empire.

CHAPTER SIX

Everywhere Ceres looked on the Isle Beyond the Mist, she saw things that made her stop and stare at their strange beauty. Hawks with rainbow-colored feathers spun as they hunted things below, but were in turn hunted by a winged serpent that eventually settled on a spire of white marble.

She walked over the emerald grass of the island, and it seemed as if she knew exactly where she had to go. She'd seen herself in her vision, there atop the hill in the distance, where rainbow-colored towers stuck up like the spines of some great beast.

Flowers grew from the low rises on the way, and Ceres reached down to touch them. When her fingers brushed them, though, their petals were of paper-thin stone. Had someone carved them that fine, or were they somehow living rock? Just the fact that she could imagine that possibility told her how strange this place was.

Ceres kept walking, heading for the spot where she knew, where she hoped, her mother would be waiting.

She reached the lower slopes of the hill and started to climb. Around her, the island was full of life. Bees buzzed in the low grass. A creature like a deer, but with crystal tines where its antlers should have been, looked at Ceres for a long time before springing away.

Yet she saw no people there, despite the buildings that dotted the landscape around her. The ones closest to Ceres had a pristine, empty feel, like a room that had been stepped out from only moments before. Ceres kept going, up toward the top of the hill, to the spot where the towers formed a circle around a broad area of grass, letting her look out between them over the whole of the rest of the island.

Yet she didn't look that way. Instead, Ceres found herself staring at the center of the circle, where a single figure stood in a robe of pure white. Unlike her vision, the figure wasn't fuzzy or out of focus. She was there, as clear and real as Ceres was. Ceres stepped forward, almost to within touching distance. There was only one person it could be.

"Mother?"

"Ceres."

The robed figure threw herself forward at the same instant Ceres did, and they met in a crushing hug that seemed to express all the things Ceres didn't know how to say: how much she'd been looking forward to this moment, how much love there was there, how incredible it was to meet this woman she'd only met in a vision.

"I knew you would come," the woman, her *mother,* said as they stepped back, "but even knowing it is different from actually *seeing* you."

She pulled back the hood of her robe then, and it seemed almost impossible that this woman could be her mother. Her sister, perhaps, because she shared the same hair, the same features. It was almost like looking into a mirror for Ceres. Yet she seemed too young to be Ceres's mother.

"I don't understand," Ceres said. "You *are* my mother?"

"I am." She reached out to hug Ceres again. "I know it must seem strange, but it's true. My kind can live a long time. I am Lycine."

A name. Ceres finally had a name for her mother. Somehow, that meant more than all the rest of it put together. Just that was enough to make the journey worth it. She wanted to stand there and just stare at her mother forever. Even so, she had questions. So many that they spilled out in a rush.

"What is this place?" she asked. "Why are you here alone? Wait, what do you mean 'your kind'?"

Lycine smiled and sat down on the grass. Ceres joined her, and as she sat, she realized that it wasn't just grass. She could see fragments of stone beneath it, arranged in mosaic form, but long since covered over by the meadow around them.

"There's no easy way to answer all of your questions," Lycine said. "Especially not when I have so many questions of my own, about you, about your life. About everything, Ceres. But I'll try. Shall we do this the old way? A question for a question?"

Ceres didn't know what to say to that, but it seemed her mother wasn't done yet.

"Do they still tell the stories of the Ancient Ones, out in the world?"

"Yes," Ceres said. She'd always paid more attention to the stories of combatlords and their exploits in the Stade, but she knew some of what they said about the Ancient Ones: the ones who had come before humanity, who sometimes looked the same and sometimes looked like so much more. Who'd built so much and then lost it. "Wait, are you saying that you're—"

"One of the Ancient Ones, yes," Lycine replied. "This was one of our places, before... well, there are some things that it is still best not to talk about. Besides, I'm owed an answer. So tell me what

29

your life has been like. I couldn't be there, but I spent so long trying to imagine what it would be like for you."

Ceres did her best, even though she didn't know where to start. She told Lycine about growing up around her father's forge, about her brothers. She told her about the rebellion, and about the Stade. She even managed to tell her about Rexus and Thanos, though those words came out choking and fractured.

"Oh, darling," her mother said, laying a hand over hers. "I wish I could have spared you some of that pain. I wish I could have been there for you."

"Why couldn't you?" Ceres asked. "Have you been here all this time?"

"I have," Lycine said. "This used to be one of the places of my people, in the old days. The others left it behind. Even I did, for a time, but these past years it has been a kind of sanctuary. And a place to wait, of course."

"To wait?" Ceres asked. "You mean for me?"

She saw her mother nod.

"People talk about seeing destiny as if it were a gift," Lycine said, "but there is a kind of prison to it, too. Understand what must happen, and you lose the choices that come with not knowing, no matter how much you might wish..." Her mother shook her head, and Ceres could see the sadness there. "This isn't the time for regret. I have my daughter here, and there is only so much time for you to learn what you came for."

She smiled and took Ceres's hand.

"Walk with me."

***

Ceres felt like days had passed while she and her mother walked the magical isle. It was breathtaking, this vista, being here with her mother. It all felt like a dream.

As they walked, they spoke mostly of the power. Her mother tried to explain it to her, and Ceres tried to understand. The strangest thing happened: as her mother spoke, Ceres felt as if her words were actually imbuing her with the power.

Even now, as they walked, Ceres felt it rising up inside her, roiling like smoke as her mother touched her shoulder. She needed to learn to control it, she'd come here to learn to control it, but compared to meeting her mother, it didn't seem important.

"Our blood has given you power," Lycine said. "The islanders tried to help unlock it, didn't they?"

Ceres thought of Eoin, and of all the strange exercises he'd had her doing. "Yes."

"For people not of our blood, they understand the world well," her mother said. "But there are things even they can't show you. Have you made anything stone yet? It's one of my talents, so I would guess it will be one of yours."

"Made things stone?" Ceres asked. She didn't understand. "So far, I've moved things. I've been faster and stronger. And—"

She didn't want to finish that. She didn't want her mother to think badly of her.

"And your power has killed things that have tried to harm you?" Lycine said.

Ceres nodded.

"Do not be ashamed of that, daughter. I have only seen a little of you, but I know what you are destined to be. You are a fine person. All that I could hope. As for making things stone…"

They stopped in a meadow of purple and yellow flowers and Ceres watched her mother pluck a small flower from the meadow, with delicate, silken petals. Through the contact with her mother, she felt the way the power flickered within her, feeling familiar but much more directed, crafted, shaped.

Stone spread across the flower like frost over a window, but it wasn't just on the surface. A second after it had begun, it was over, and her mother held one of the stone flowers Ceres had seen lower on the island.

"Did you feel it?" Lycine asked.

Ceres nodded. "But how did you do it?"

"Feel again." She plucked another flower, and this time it was impossibly slow as she turned it to something with marble petals and a granite stem. Ceres tried to track the movement of the power within her, and it was as though her own moved in response, trying to copy it.

"Good," Lycine said. "Your blood knows. Now you try."

She passed a flower to Ceres. Ceres reached down, concentrating as she tried to grasp the power within her and push it into the form she'd felt her mother's take.

The flower exploded.

"Well," Lycine said with a laugh, "*that* was unexpected."

It was so different from the way the mother she'd grown up with would have reacted. She'd beaten Ceres for the least failure. Lycine just passed her another flower.

"Relax," she said. "You already know how it should feel. Take that feeling. Imagine it. Make it real."

31

Ceres tried to do it, thinking about what she'd felt when her mother had transformed her flower. She took the feeling and filled it with power the way her father might have filled a mold at the forge with iron.

"Open your eyes, Ceres," Lycine said.

Ceres hadn't even realized that she'd closed them until her mother said the words. She forced herself to look, even though right then she was afraid to. Once she'd looked, she stared, because she could barely believe it. She held a single, perfectly formed, petrified bloom, transformed into something like basalt by her power.

"I did that?" Ceres asked. Even with everything else she could do, it still seemed nearly impossible.

"You did," her mother said, and Ceres could hear the pride there. "Now we just need to get you to do it without your eyes closed."

That took longer, and a lot more flowers. Yet Ceres found herself enjoying the practice. More than that, every time her mother smiled at her efforts, Ceres felt a burst of love expanding through her. Even as the minutes spilled into hours, she kept going.

"Yes," her mother said at last, "that's perfect."

It was more than that; it was easy. Easy to reach out and pull power from inside her. Easy to channel it. Easy to leave behind a perfectly preserved stone flower. It was only as the rush of doing it faded that Ceres realized just how tired she was.

"It's all right," her mother said, taking her hand. "Your power takes energy and effort. Even the strongest of us could only do so much at once." She smiled. "But your power knows what it is for now. It will rise up when someone threatens you, or when you summon it to you. It will do more, too."

Ceres sensed a flicker of power from her mother, and she could see the full potential of her power. She saw the stone buildings and gardens in a new light, as things that had been built with that power, crafted in ways no human could understand. She felt full, somehow. Complete.

Some of the happiness seemed to fade from her mother's expression. Ceres heard her sigh.

"What is it?" Ceres asked.

"I just wish that we had more time together," Lycine said. "I would love to walk you through the towers here and tell you the history of my people. I would love to hear all about this Thanos you loved so much, and show you the gardens where the sun has never touched the trees."

"Then do it," Ceres said. She felt as though she might have stayed there forever. "Show me all of it. Tell me about the past. Tell me about my father, and what happened when I was born."

Her mother shook her head though.

"That is one thing you aren't ready for yet. As for time, I told you before that destiny can be a prison, darling, and you have a bigger destiny than most."

"I've seen flashes of it," Ceres admitted, thinking of the dreams that had come to her again and again on the boat."

"Then you know why we can't stay here and be a family, no matter how much either of us might wish it," her mother said. "Although maybe the future holds time for that. That and more."

"First, though, I have to go back, don't I?" Ceres said.

Her mother nodded.

"You do," she said. "You must return, Ceres. Return and free Delos from the Empire, as you were always meant to do."

CHAPTER SEVEN

It was hard for Stephania to believe that she'd already been married to Thanos for six weeks. Yet with the feast of the Blood Moon here, that was how long it had been. Six weeks of bliss, every one as wonderful as she could have hoped for.

"You look amazing," she said, looking over at Thanos in the rooms they now shared in the castle. He was a vision in deep red silk, set off with red gold and rubies. She could hardly believe that he was hers, some days. "Red suits you."

"It makes me look as though I'm covered in blood," Thanos replied.

"Which is rather the point, given that it's the Blood Moon," Stephania pointed out. She leaned in to kiss him. She liked being able to do that when she wanted. If there were more time, she might have taken the moment to do a lot more.

"It hardly matters what I wear though," Thanos said. "There's no one in the room who will be looking at me when you're there beside me."

Perhaps another man could have put the compliment more elegantly, but there was something about the earnest way Thanos said it that meant more to Stephania than all the perfectly judged poems in the world.

Besides, she *had* worked rather hard on picking out the most beautiful dress in Delos. It shimmered in shades of red like a flame wrapped around her. She'd even bribed the dressmaker to ensure that the original, destined for a minor noblewoman lower in the city, was irretrievably delayed.

Stephania offered her arm, and Thanos took it, escorting her down toward the great feast hall where they'd had their wedding. Was it already six weeks that they'd been married? Six weeks of more bliss than Stephania could have believed, living together in apartments set aside for them by the queen within the castle. There were even rumors that the king was planning to bestow a new estate on Thanos, a little way from the city. For six weeks, they'd been the most watched couple in the city, lauded wherever they went. Stephania had enjoyed that.

"Do remember not to punch Lucious when you see him tonight," Stephania said.

"I've managed to keep from doing it so far," Thanos replied. "Don't worry."

Stephania did worry, though. She didn't want to risk losing Thanos now that she had him as her husband. She didn't want to find him executed for attacking the heir to the throne, and not just because of the position it would put her in. She might have set out to acquire him for a husband for the prestige it would bring, but now... now she was surprised to find that she loved him.

"Prince Thanos and his wife, Lady Stephania!" the herald at the door announced, and Stephania smiled, leaning her head against Thanos's shoulder. She always loved hearing that.

She looked around the room. For their wedding, it had been arranged in white, but now it shone in red and black. The wine in the glasses was a thick blood red, the feast tables had meat left just on the edge of bloody, and every noble in the place wore the colors of the shifting moon.

Stephania walked on Thanos's arm, parsing the relationships there, keeping track of the latest intrigues even as she simply enjoyed being seen. Was that Lady Christina, slipping off into the shadows to talk to a merchant prince from the Far Islands? Was Isolde's daughter wearing fewer jewels than usual?

Of course, she saw Lucious drinking too much, eating too much, and eyeing the women. Briefly, Stephania thought his eyes flickered to hers, his look one that would have guaranteed a fight if Thanos had seen it. It was a pity, really, that her attempt to poison him at the wedding feast had gone so badly. If Thanos hadn't made him so angry that he'd crushed his wine glass, then Lucious would have gone to sleep that night and not woken. It would have been done.

Since then, there had been no opportunity to deal with him. The usual people she might have employed were being more cautious now that the one she'd used for Thanos had gone missing, and the trick with killing was never the act of it; it was always doing it in such a way that people didn't suspect. There had simply never been a chance to get close to Lucious without it being obvious.

"Ah, Prince Thanos," a white-whiskered man said, approaching them both, "Lady Stephania. You make such a wonderful couple!"

Stephania searched her memory for the man, coming up with the answer effortlessly. "General Haven, you're too kind. How is your wife doing?"

"Happy enough to spend my gold on new necklaces. I take it you'll be keeping Prince Thanos from the new expedition to Haylon?"

"There's a new expedition?" Thanos said. Stephania could hear the curiosity there. It was obviously the first her husband had heard of it.

"Heading out tomorrow," General Haven said. "I tried to persuade his majesty to let me head this one, but he decided on Olliant instead."

Probably because the man was capable of organizing something more than a long-winded speech. Stephania had heard that Haven had once been a competent general, but now he hung onto his role only through his connections.

"Well," Stephania said, "I'm sure your wife will be happy to have you home. I know I'm glad that Thanos isn't going anywhere."

The old man drifted away, and Stephania turned to Thanos.

"We should go and mingle," Stephania said. "I should go and hear all the gossip the women of the court have to tell, and tell them how glorious their choices of dress are. *You* should go and pay your respects to the king. People have been muttering about how little you've been there for formal audiences lately."

"I've just been busy," Thanos said. "Enjoying married life, for a start."

Stephania knew her husband better than that. She still laughed though. "I've been enjoying it too, but you know you can't afford to offend the king. Think of it as a game, Thanos. A big game, where the prize is getting to live happily, and where you don't get a choice if you play."

"Is that what you do?" Thanos asked.

Stephania spread her hands. "Why do you think I'm about to go and tell General Haven's wife how lovely her new necklace is?" She kissed his cheek. "Please, Thanos. I love how honest you are, but whatever happened when you spoke to the king, you can't get on his bad side."

"I'll try," Thanos said, heading off in the direction of the king and queen.

Stephania watched him go. She loved watching him. Even as she started making her way through the room, she kept glancing back to keep an eye on where Thanos had gotten to. She'd never thought that she would be like this, giddy as a milkmaid swooning over him. But that was love, and Stephania wasn't going to allow anything to jeopardize things.

"Do we have any information on the boy, Sartes, yet?" Stephania asked one of her handmaids in a whisper. She made sure that none of them ever knew all of her affairs, but she also made sure that she picked clever girls, drawn up from the lower end of the acceptable classes. Girls who would owe her everything, in other words.

"We know that after his escape from the army, he joined up with the rebellion," the handmaid said. "I believe I know which group, my lady."

"Well done," Stephania said, with a brief touch of her hand bestowed like a blessing. "Go to Captain Var and tell him that I want the boy in chains."

"Yes, my lady."

The girl hurried off. Captain Var was a necessary evil. The mercenary was a lecher and a torturer, but curiously, he was surprisingly loyal, and he was good at the… specialized jobs Stephania had him perform. Probably it helped that Stephania was in a position to outbid everyone else for his services. At least one would-be rival had found herself disappearing into the slave pits thanks to the good captain's graces.

Stephania continued her smiling way around the feast, sampling a bite of food here, a sip of wine there as she moved from acquaintance to rival to would-be friend, never stopping long in one place, never letting her eyes stray from Thanos for long.

Perhaps she shouldn't be making such an issue of Ceres's younger brother. If he hadn't already died in one of the rebellion's raids, he almost certainly would soon. Even if he lived, did it really matter?

It did. Just the thought of it was enough to make Stephania dig her nails into her palms, bringing with it a sharp stab of pain. The boy was no threat in himself. Stephania bore him no ill will, but just the fact that he existed was a connection to the memory of Ceres. Stephania could *not* allow her to intrude on her marriage. Not in life, and not in death. No, she had to be certain, whatever it took.

Stephania looked over to Thanos again. He seemed to be done with the king, and she wanted to dance with him now. She wanted to draw him close to her and feel the strength of him pressed up against her. She wanted to remind all those there that she had gained the greatest prize worth taking. Above all, she wanted to fill his thoughts so full of her that there could never be any room for Ceres ever again.

She started to make her way over toward him, but she only got a little of the way there before she started to feel so sick that her head swam. Had she been poisoned? No, she couldn't have been. She was always careful about what she ate and who she took it

37

from. She consumed antidotes every morning, and she knew better than anyone what to taste and smell for.

Even so, she found herself stumbling in the direction of the courtyard. One of her maids helped her, and Stephania found herself leaning on the girl more than she would have liked. The night air was cool, but it didn't really help.

"Are you all right, my lady?" the maid asked as they got out there.

Stephania wanted to snap that of course she wasn't, but her body chose that moment to betray her and she vomited. It tasted foul, but Stephania was mostly just glad that she'd gotten out of the hall before anyone saw. Her maid held her hair back.

"I don't know what's happening," Stephania said. "It can't be poison. It *can't.*"

"My lady," the maid said, "is it… is it possible that you're pregnant?"

Stephania wanted to tell the girl not to be stupid, but it fit, didn't it? Could she be? Was it possible? She stood there in shock, trying to think as she cleaned herself up with her maid's help. It had never occurred to her that she might be pregnant. It had just seemed so much more obvious in her world that she might have been attacked by some enemy.

"Tell no one about this," Stephania said. "Go back to the feast. If anyone asks you where I am, say that I felt unwell and returned to my rooms. Fail and I'll have you skinned, do you understand?"

"Yes, my lady," the girl said, looking frightened.

Stephania offset that with a hug. "Thank you. I should have thought of it myself."

She hurried through the castle, but even so, it took her a while to find the chambers of the royal apothecary. In general, if Stephania needed a potion or a poultice, she was more than capable of putting it together herself. Yet this wasn't something she kept the materials for, and she didn't want to waste her time with the toads and rabbits of so-called wise women.

Of course, when Stephania got there, the door was locked, the apothecary away. Thankfully, the lock was a poor one, easy to force open even though Stephania rarely stooped to such things for herself.

She made her way inside, looking through the jars of powders and herbs. It was dangerous, working with someone else's stocks, but Stephania thought that she could recognize what she needed. There were enough ladies of the court having enough affairs to need to know these things, and it seemed the apothecary kept vials made up.

Stephania found one and used it, ignoring the embarrassment of doing so in the middle of the place. She stared at the clear solution with impatience, waiting to see what would happen next.

When it slowly shifted to blue, Stephania felt a rush of feelings spreading through her. Shock, because she'd never expected this. Apprehension for all that might happen next. Above all, though, there was joy. Joy for one simple fact:

She was having Thanos's child.

CHAPTER EIGHT

The morning after the feast, Thanos rose quietly and sneaked his way through the rooms he shared with Stephania. He'd learned to be careful after she'd followed him to hunt Lucious.

"Let her sleep," Thanos said to one of Stephania's maids as he passed. "I'm just going down to the training ground ahead of the Killings later, and Stephania looked a little tired after the feast last night."

"Yes, Prince Thanos," the maid said.

Thanos set off in the direction of the training grounds, because that was a believable place for him to go this early. He needn't have worried. The castle was quiet. Servants bustled about their work, but the nobles who might have been in a position to question him were all still in bed. After the feast last night, it was exactly what Thanos had been hoping for.

Because of what he'd heard last night. What General Haven had said was just the start. With the wine flowing and so many nobles gathered in one place, Stephania hadn't been the only one listening to gossip. The only difference was that Thanos had been listening with a point, taking in anything that might help the rebels.

He hurried along the corridors of the castle, heading for the offices of the royal chamberlain. They had probably been grand once, but were now piled so high with records and missives that the only effect was of chaos. There was a minor official sitting at a table there, but no sign of the man himself. He was probably sleeping off the effects of the feast like everyone else.

"Can I help you, Prince Thanos?" the official asked.

Thanos silently apologized for how difficult he was about to make the other man's day. It was the only way he could think of.

"Where is the Lord Chamberlain?" Thanos demanded in his best "spoiled noble" voice. He'd modeled it on Lucious.

"Forgive me, but his lordship is feeling a little ill this—"

"I didn't ask how he was," Thanos snapped. "I asked *where* he was. I need to discuss details of the estates the king is considering giving to me and my wife, because I want to make sure that it's suitable for Stephania."

"Perhaps I could—"

"Are you the Lord Chamberlain?" Thanos asked, then paused. "I'm sorry. It's just that I want this to be perfect before Stephania hears the details. Would you please fetch him?"

The official hurried off. Thanos hoped he wouldn't hurry too much as he shut and locked the door behind him, because he needed the time.

As quickly as he could, he found pen, ink, and parchment, trying to remember what he could of the usual forms. His Majesty, King of Delos, ruler of the Empire... Thanos did his best to keep the letters sharp and official looking. How long would he have to write everything he needed?

He found the chamberlain's copy of the royal seal, and set wax to melt. Thanos could imagine the official running, the Lord Chamberlain dressing in a hurry. Even so, he couldn't rush the writing more. It had to look just right. The king did not rush commands like this. He sent them with full majesty, knowing that others would wait for him.

Thanos could hear footsteps now, along with arguing voices. He reached for the seal, dripping wax down onto the parchment.

"You couldn't deal with this yourself?"

"The prince insisted!"

"Even so, you could have found a way! And now the door is shut. The key."

Thanos pressed the seal down into the soft wax, putting it back into place as quickly as he dared. There was no time to do more. He just had time to hide the parchment he'd worked on before the Lord Chamberlain came blustering in, smiling with the lack of warmth of a man who had just been roused from his bed too soon.

"Prince Thanos, it is an honor. What can I do for you this fine morning?"

The hardest part was spending fifteen long minutes discussing details of estates and stables, farms and river rights, when Thanos knew just how little time he might have before it was too late. Finally, it felt as though he was able to smile and make his exit.

"Thank you for all this," he said. "Now that you've gone through it with me, I see that there was no reason to worry. I will leave you to your work."

He forced himself to walk as made his way through the castle, heading for the tower where they kept their messenger birds: rock doves and homing pigeons, ravens and occasional larger birds. Every outpost of the Empire regularly sent its birds, well trained to know where their homes were. There was no one minding the entrance yet, but Thanos was still cautious. There might be someone above by now.

He crept up among the birds, moving quietly, with every creak of the boards below his feet making him pause. Thanos hoped that

41

no one was up there feeding the birds, because he wasn't sure what lie he would be able to tell them. There wasn't, though, and Thanos made his way over to the cages where the birds for Haylon, large black ravens, were kept. They looked as though they hadn't flown in a while.

Thanos picked one out and attached a message to its leg. It wasn't much more than a hurried warning, along with a promise to do what he could. He didn't dare sign it, but hopefully, Akila and the other rebels would know who it was from and trust it.

Now for the more dangerous part of his plan, and the one where he had to hurry the most. Thanos practically ran in the direction of the stables, saddling his horse and riding toward the docks at a full gallop. Around him, the city was already waking up. Servants and wives were emptying chamber pots into the streets, hawkers were calling out their wares, while carts were making their way through the streets.

Thanos had to dodge them all as he raced down over the cobbles, following the scent of sea air. The docks were busier than the rest of the city put together. Fishermen were landing their catches or heading out. A merchant ship was unloading with the aid of a string of porters.

And what was left of the Empire's navy sat low in the water, laden down with troops. It was a motley collection of ships compared to the first invasion force, hastily repurposed pleasure craft and cargo ships obvious among the war galleys. Thanos ran his horse down to the water's edge. This was more public than he wanted, but it couldn't be helped.

"Where is General Olliant?" he called out to a group of soldiers. When they pointed to a ship still being loaded by the docks, he handed his reins to one of them and ran up the gangplank. Sailors started to move in front of him, but they obviously recognized Thanos, because they quickly stepped back.

Thanos spotted the general by his golden armor and hurried over to him on the top deck. The general saluted.

"Prince Thanos," the general said. "I wasn't aware that you were to travel with us."

"I'm not," Thanos said. "But it seems you aren't going anywhere either, General."

He held out the parchment he'd prepared. He only wished he'd had more time to work on it. Was the ink even dry yet?

"What's this?" General Olliant asked.

"New orders," Thanos said. "General Haven is to be given command of this expedition."

"Haven?" The shock in the general's voice was obvious. Thanos could understand it. Haven was a long way from the dynamic, ruthless general that would be needed to crush Haylon. That was the point. "This is my expedition!"

"The king requires you elsewhere, General."

The general tore open the orders Thanos had forged, staring at them. Thanos's heart beat faster as he did it, tracking every movement of the man's eyes. Thanos saw him trace the outline of the seal.

"This is still warm," General Olliant said, "and why is the king sending you with messages, your highness?"

Thanos could hear the suspicion there. At any moment, the man might decide to send a runner to the castle to find out what was happening. Thanos couldn't let that happen.

"That just shows how urgent it is," Thanos said. He lowered his voice. "And there's more to it. Do you trust the men around you?"

The general glanced around, then took a step back from his men before dropping his voice to match Thanos's. "What is it?" he demanded. "What is this all about?"

"You're not going to Haylon because the king has a crucial task for you," Thanos said. "We think we know where the leaders of the rebellion are going to be meeting, but we need a general with the skills to handle the task."

He saw General Olliant's eyes shine with interest. "I'll go back to the castle then, and gather—"

"There's no time," Thanos said quickly. "If you have men here you can trust, take them, but unless we act now, we'll miss them. There's a force waiting for your orders in the Glass Spur pass, but if you don't ride hard, you'll never get there before the leaders move on from their meeting."

"I'll go at once," General Olliant promised, and he was almost faster down the gangplank than Thanos was. Thanos knew it was the desire for glory that had him moving so fast, not the thought of new orders, but it was enough.

Thanos rode back in the direction of the castle. Now he just had to tell General Haven about his new position, but he suspected that wouldn't be a problem. After all, the man had already hinted that he wanted this. It would simply look as though Thanos had interceded.

As he rode, his mind went to the risks he'd taken this morning. Could he ensure that no one found out? The army was about to take off in the direction of Haylon, and so those who had seen him at the docks wouldn't be able to talk about what he'd done. Of course, there was the problem of what might happen when General Olliant discovered there was no force of soldiers waiting for him, but maybe Thanos could kill two birds with one stone there. Maybe he could send the rebellion news of where one of the Empire's generals was going to be relatively unguarded. He was almost back at the castle. Now he—

"Thanos? Is that you?"

Thanos cursed silently as he turned in the saddle to see Lucious walking out of one of the side streets near the entrance, along with a small group of hangers-on.

"Lucious," Thanos said, forcing a smile. "You're up early."

"Up early?" Lucious countered, and now Thanos could hear the faint slur to his words. "A real man doesn't sleep on a festival night! At least, not in his own bed. Talking of beds, have you tired of the lovely Stephania already? Or maybe she's tired of you? Maybe she's gone out looking for a real man, and you're going after her?"

His cronies laughed along with him, of course.

"Just out for a morning ride, Lucious," Thanos said. "You should try it."

"As I recall," Lucious said, "the last time you went out for a morning ride, you ended up betraying the Empire for some peasants. What are you up to this time?"

"Oh, go get some sleep," Thanos snapped back, but inside, his stomach knotted. "You're too drunk to be worth talking to."

"You're hiding something, and I'll find out what," Lucious promised.

Thanos waved it away, but it was probably just as well Lucious was drunk, or he'd see the way Thanos paled.

"I'll see you at the Killings later, Lucious. For now, I have better things to do."

Like persuading an incompetent general to take over the Empire's biggest military operation, telling the rebels about General Olliant, and finding a way to do it all without Lucious finding out more than he should.

44

CHAPTER NINE

Anka forced herself to stay still and watch while below, in the Stade, men died in honor of the Blood Moon. Two muscled southerners fought, their blades flickering, while the crowd bayed with every spray of red that stained the sands.

There was more red spread throughout the terraces. People wore whatever they had in the Blood Moon's colors, and some threw red dust and dye into the air, covering even those who'd come in normal clothes. Anka had plenty on her, but she was already wearing an elaborate red costume, complete with long-nosed mask.

It made it easier to hide the weapons.

Below her, the fight continued out on the sands, with the clang and clash of blades lost in the shouts of the people around her. There were only a few nobles up in the royal enclosure today, dressed in ways that made the simple red tunics of most of the crowd look like children copying their parents. They wore silk and rubies, reclined on deep red couches, and drank red wine from crystal goblets. It was a pity there weren't more. If the king had been there, they could have brought down the Empire.

Anka signaled to other figures costumed in the colors of the Blood Moon, watching them start to slip through the crowd around her. They all had their jobs. Anka had planned every step of this, but there were some things you couldn't account for, especially in a place like this.

"Hey, watch yourself!" a man said as Anka started to push her way through the crowd. He reached out for her, and Anka felt him pull back as she drew a knife. There wasn't any time for trouble. She had to keep moving.

"Sorry, excuse me," Anka said, picking her way through. She could see the others moving and pick out the patterns there. She just hoped that none of the guards in the Stade could.

Ahead, she could see the gates that led down underneath the Stade, into the spaces where the combatlords were kept. There were large guards on the door, there to keep the crowds back. One put a hand up as Anka approached.

"Get back," he said. "If you want to see the combatlords, you'll have to wait, the same as anyone else."

"Get out of my way, and you won't be harmed," Anka said.

"Won't be harmed?" the guard said with a laugh. "What do you think you're going to do?"

"This," Anka said, and pulled away her costume, revealing the armor underneath. "For the rebellion!"

"For the rebellion!" voices called around her. "Down with the Empire!"

Other figures rushed forward, casting off their disguises, drawing daggers and clubs. They overwhelmed the guards at the gate in seconds. Berin was there with Sartes, breaking open the locks with forge hammers and rushing inside. Anka went with them, down into the space beneath the Stade, rushing for the next set of gates, the next group of guards.

Those stood just beyond another set of iron doors, armed with the clubs and whips and swords they would need to control unruly combatlords. Anka could see the dank, cruel conditions beyond, and guess at some of the horrors there. It gave her the strength she needed to lift a crossbow and fire through the bars.

Others fired with her, and the guards went down. She saw Oreth working on the lock, and then they were inside. Now they had to fight, because the Empire wasn't going to leave just a few guards to control so many dangerous slaves. A guard ran at her, sword cutting down, and Anka barely sidestepped in time.

He cut again, and Anka managed to get the body of her crossbow in the way. She stabbed with the knife in her other hand, moving in close as she struck once, then again. She felt the blade go into her attacker, and he fell. She saw Sartes and Berin struggling with another guard, bringing him down with hammer blows.

Around her, guards were dying. The space under the Stade was formidable, the guards strong and powerfully built, but their whole system was designed for controlling threats from the inside, not keeping out attackers from the world beyond. Who would want to attack a space full of combatlords? Who would want to free slaves?

Anka would.

She strode into the space beneath the Stade and looked around at the combatlords there with their weapon carriers and trainers. Some were in their armor, some were in chains, while a few were receiving massages as their trainers sought to prepare them. They were pampered in some ways. Anka was just hoping that they understood that freedom still mattered more.

Berin spoke first. It was what they'd agreed; the only way this might work. "Listen up, lads. You all know me. I made weapons for you long enough. Now, I'm bringing you something better: the chance of freedom. All you have to do is listen."

He stepped aside, and it was time for Anka to step forward.

"I am Anka, the leader of the rebellion," Anka said as she stepped into the middle of them. She could see them sizing her up, and a flicker of fear passed through her at the thought of what might happen if these men decided that she was somehow unworthy.

"What are you doing here?" one asked. He was a black-bearded giant of a man, thick with muscle.

"We're here to free you," Anka said.

"Free us?" the combatlord countered. "*You're* here to free *us*?"

He laughed, and Anka knew she had to act fast.

"Maybe you don't want to be free," she said, raising her voice. "Maybe you like your time here. Maybe you like having everything you want provided for you, with nothing to do but train, and fight…" She paused for a second. "And die, of course."

She looked around at them. At all of them down there in the cool half-dark. "That's what it means, being a combatlord. You fight, and you're told it's for honor or for glory, but deep down, you know the truth. You fight because you aren't given a choice. Even the ones of you who are free don't really have the choice to walk away, because there's too much riding on every match."

"And you're going to give us more?" the bearded combatlord asked.

Anka shook her head. "You're going to take it for yourselves. The nobles above treat you like playthings. They wager on you and they sell you, they take the applause when you win and cast you aside the moment you lose. They might give you a few luxuries, but let's not pretend they care about you."

"So what do you want us to do?" another combatlord asked.

Anka smiled, because she knew she had them. "Rise up. Fight for *everyone*. It's what they've trained you to do, but they've never given you anything worth fighting for. Fight with us, and that's what you'll have. You can fight to be free. You can fight for all the people out there. With us, you can fight to bring down the Empire!"

That brought a cheer from the men there, and several were already reaching for the weapons they would have used in the Stade.

"More guards are coming," Oreth called from near the doors. "It looks as though they know what's going on."

"Let them come," one of the combatlords said, but Anka didn't want to fight there. This whole space was designed to put those within at a disadvantage.

"Up!" she ordered. "Up to the Stade!"

To her astonishment, even the combatlords did as she said, pouring up toward the sands together. They burst out onto the floor of the Stade, but Anka didn't waste any time blinking in the sunlight. Instead, she raised her dagger, hoping it caught the sunlight.

"People of Delos! We are the rebellion, and we are here to free you!"

There was no time to say more than that, because guards were already pouring onto the sands of the Stade from the other side. There were so many that Anka could barely count them all; far more than their own small force. It might have been some horribly mismatched contest in the Killings, except this was about more than the entertainment of the crowd. Much more.

There was no time for clever planning, and they couldn't sit there waiting for the soldiers to attack them in perfect formation, so Anka did the only thing she could do.

"Charge!"

She ran at the head of the group, not knowing if anyone would follow her. She closed in on the guards there, who stood with shields up and spears extended. Anka could imagine herself impaled on those spears all too easily.

Then the combatlords surged past her, and she got to see firsthand that Sartes had been right. They were better than any soldier could have been. Anka had seen them fighting one another before, and the evenness of it had disguised just how dangerous they were. Against anyone normal, they seemed barely human.

She saw one leap over the wall of shields, stabbing downward as he passed over a guard. Another spun spiked chains, ripping spears out of the hands of their wielders. The bearded fighter struck with a trident, thrusting it through one soldier before knocking another back with the haft.

Anka found herself plunged into the middle of the fight, and it was chaos. A soldier got near her, so she stabbed at him, but the fight swept them apart again. A sword came at her head, and she found a sword interposed. Sartes nodded to her as Anka stabbed at the soldier who'd struck.

The combatlords were like whirlwinds in the middle of the fight. Each fought alone, an island of violence surrounded by opponents, but it didn't seem to make any difference. The rebels fought like small fish following in the wake of sharks, darting in and out of the fight, filling in the gaps left by their mayhem. They were more evenly matched with the soldiers, but with the combatlords there, it seemed to be enough.

For now, at least. Anka knew there would be more coming. She pulled back from the fight, standing on the sands and staring up at the crowd.

"We are the rebellion, but so are you!" Anka called out. "If you want to be free, you must take that freedom!" She pointed at the balcony where the nobles were already starting to flee. "Look at them! The Empire has oppressed you for too long! Help to fight it now!"

Many people kept staring down as though it was all a show, but many more responded. The crowd surged as people started toward guards at the gates, or struggled to get to the nobles above. Anka saw people starting to fight; against guards, against those who wanted the Empire to stand, or simply to get away.

She threw herself back into the fight in the Stade as she saw Edrin struggling with a soldier. She kicked out, knocking the man off balance, and Edrin lashed out with his sword. Anka saw a group of guards trying to re-form their shield wall, and she didn't have the strength to do more than point, charging again and knowing this time that the others would follow.

The battle swirled around Anka like a living thing. She did what she could, looking for openings to attack even though she knew she could never keep up with the capabilities of the combatlords. She saw people fighting and dying in every direction, men and women, combatlords and soldiers, rebels and people who had joined them from the crowd.

Above it all, Anka heard one noise she had hoped not to hear when she arrived: the sound of horns. It meant that they'd run out of time. They'd done what they'd come there to do, but now they needed to find a way out of there before it fell apart around them.

The Stade was in uproar now, with the people there in full revolt. It should have been a sight to fill Anka with hope.

Even so, the sound of the horns only brought dread with it.

More soldiers were coming, more than they could ever dream to battle.

And they had no way out.

CHAPTER TEN

Ceres left the Isle Beyond the Mist behind with a heavy heart. She didn't want to go, however much she might need to, however much her destiny might lie on the mainland. Her mother was on the island.

But her mother had been the one to insist that Ceres go, even if there had been tears in her eyes while she did it. She'd been the one to load fresh supplies onto Ceres's boat, and to point her on the bearing she needed to take to return to the mainland. She'd stood on the beach, not waving, but watching, while Ceres sailed off. She'd been there as a tiny figure on the beach until finally Ceres had been too far away to make her out. Possibly she had still been there even when the mist closed around her.

The journey back through the mist was less eerie than it had been coming there, but this time, Ceres could feel the power in the fog surrounding her. Eoin had said that this was somewhere for her to go alone. *Could* anyone else have made it through with her? How many people blundered into this barrier and didn't come out?

When she made it through, it was daytime, but somehow the world didn't seem quite as vibrant as it did on the other side. It was like stepping into another, slightly more leaden, reality, where the glorious homes of the Ancient Ones couldn't be imagined except as stories.

She sailed on, keeping the tiller of her small boat lashed to the course her mother had set and focusing on catching the wind with the boat's sail. There was a fresh breeze behind her, pushing her along, but even so, Ceres didn't know how long it would take her to return.

She thought of everything that might be waiting for her there. The rebellion was there, and she didn't know how well it was doing. Perhaps it had already won, or already been wiped out. That thought made her chest tighten, because her father and her brother would be with the rebellion, if they were anywhere. No, she had to believe that they were all right.

Ceres wasn't sure what she was going to be able to do once she got there. She knew more of who she was now, but not everything. She had more control of the powers within her. Would it be enough? Ceres thought of Thanos, dead on the beaches of Haylon, and of all the people who suffered under the Empire. She would *make* it enough, even if she had to walk into the throne room of the Empire and turn the king to stone in front of everyone.

Ceres watched the waves around her boat for a while, and she realized that they were growing, forming into a swell that buffeted the small craft despite its construction. The boat was moving faster too, and Ceres could feel the wind ripping at the sails, shoving her craft along roughly through the peaks and troughs of the water.

She looked ahead, and her heart pounded as she saw a storm brewing.

It began as a patch of bruised sky on the horizon. It spread, seeming to fill everything ahead, and Ceres knew that there would have been no way to sail around it even if she had dared to deviate from the course her mother had set. It seemed to fill the world.

The wind soon raged in her ears, and she clutched the wood, knowing the only thing to do was hold on and hope that it wouldn't be too bad.

It was.

The first band of rain hit Ceres as solidly as a river. It pummeled her from above, while around her the rising wind howled. The first cracks of thunder sounded, deafening against the quiet of the sea, and lightning flickered among the clouds. It arced down too, and Ceres saw the water steam where it struck.

Her boat's sails billowed madly, and Ceres fought to get them down before they tore to shreds. She should have done it as soon as she saw the storm, but somehow it had felt right to press on in spite of the danger. She hauled at the ropes, using all of the strength that her blood gave her, and even then, it was a fight to keep the boom of the mast from breaking free of her grip.

In the distance, she thought she could see a waterspout rising. It spun wildly, and Ceres hoped desperately that it wouldn't come close. Her head whipped around as it stalked along like some living thing, passing close enough that Ceres could feel the massive pull of the air there.

Just that moment of distraction was enough. Ceres felt the ropes in her hand pull free fast enough to burn, and she cried out as they ripped through her palm. She heard a crack that drowned out even the thunder, and slowly, so slowly that it might have been a huge tree falling, her mast toppled into the waves.

Ceres looked at it in despair. Her boat had no oars, no way to control it without the sail, but there was nothing she could do to get it back. Tossed by the waves, without even a mast now, all she could do was hold on—as the waves grew ever higher.

A massive wave suddenly lifted her fifty, a hundred feet high. She looked over the precipice and screamed, as her entire world came crashing down.

Mother, she thought. *How could you let me die like this?*

***

Sharpness poked at the edge of Ceres's consciousness, and she woke slowly, struggling out of the depths of exhaustion into which she'd fallen. How many days had it been now? How long had she drifted? Heat and a lack of fresh water had glued her tongue to the roof of her mouth, while her eyes felt so heavy it seemed like an impossible task to open them.

Something jabbed at her again, and Ceres managed to open her eyes this time. She found herself looking up at the features of a man whose hair had been styled into elaborate spikes that were probably there to make him look more terrifying. He wore a kind of half armor of leather scraps, and the curved sword in his hand explained the sharp pain that had dragged Ceres from her sleep.

There were half a dozen more like him on her small boat, rooting through it for any scrap that might be of value. They were wild-looking men, covered in tattoos and bangles, their clothes gaudy wherever they didn't form armor. To the starboard side of Ceres's boat, the hull of a much larger galley rose like a wall punctuated by oar ports. Symbols promising pain and death were daubed on the side in paint the color of blood, leaving Ceres in no doubt about the kind of men who had woken her.

Pirates.

"She's awake," the one who'd prodded her said. "Looks like she might be worth hauling out of this boat after all."

"Could be fun for a while," another agreed. "Been a long time at sea."

"It'll be a longer time for her," a third pirate said with a laugh that made Ceres shiver.

Ceres looked up and saw more men leering over the side of the ship. Some of them catcalled and made lewd gestures. She cringed back.

"Eventually, we'll sell you to a slaver," the first pirate said with a laugh. "Eventually. And in the meantime, we're going to keep you chained in the galley for any man that wants you."

"I'll... kill you," Ceres managed through cracked lips.

That just got another laugh from him. "Oh, it's fun when they have fight in them. Hey, Nim, do you remember that barbarian woman we took? Had to tie her to the prow like a figurehead in a storm to break her. I doubt it will take that much with this one, though. Probably just a good whipping or two."

52

He reached down for Ceres, and she felt his hand close over her arm, hauling her to her feet. She tensed to fight, even though there were probably too many of them to fight all at once, given how weak she felt.

"Not so tough now, are you?" the pirate asked, casually backhanding her. Ceres tasted blood.

She also felt the power in her rising up, lashing out like a whip through her. She remembered the way she'd shaped it before, with her mother in the meadow. She felt her power jump out through the contact between her and the pirate, and she saw the stone creep out over him.

It rippled across his flesh like one of the waves around her, and he barely even had enough time to look surprised before the flow of the stone passed across his face. One moment, Ceres was faced with a pirate who wanted to attack her; the next there was a statue there that seemed like a perfect replica of the man.

It felt no different from the moment when she'd done it with the flower, but it *was* different, because until a second ago this had been a human being. Ceres had been staring into the man's eyes when the stone took them, and now they were orbs of blank marble, veined in red and looking as though they could have been carved by the greatest sculptor who ever lived.

A brief, pure sense of horror passed through Ceres at what she had just done, and yet, hadn't this man deserved it? She forced herself to composure, and looked up at the rail of the pirate vessel as she disengaged her tunic from the cold, dead grip of the statue.

The men above were staring down open-mouthed, silent now where before they had called down obscene suggestions. Ceres looked around until she found the cargo netting the men had used to clamber into her smaller boat, and climbed up it a little at a time. She still felt starved and thirsty beyond endurance, but with her power flowing through her, she more than had the strength to make the climb.

She hopped onto the deck of the pirate galley, standing in the middle of an expanding circle of the thugs there. None of them seemed to want to be the first to step toward her.

"Who leads here?" Ceres asked, finding the strength to make the words seem powerful.

"I do!" a man said, stepping forward with a sword in his hand. "And the others might be scared of your witchcraft, but I'm not."

He stepped forward, hefting the sword as if to strike at Ceres. The skills the forest folk had taught her made it easy to step aside and kick his feet from under him.

"I'll kill you," he promised. "I'll do it so slowly you beg for death."

"How many people have you hurt?" Ceres asked. "How many boats have you attacked? How many have you sold into slavery?"

She stepped aside from another blow, bringing her hand up. This time, she called the power, and the stone flowed over the pirate leader, spreading out from her hand in ripples. Before, she'd been horrified by it, but every evil thing the others there had done, this man had ordered. There were some people even Ceres couldn't feel pity for.

"Who leads here?" Ceres asked again, and the silence among the pirates was answer enough. The first of them to kneel was a relatively young one, but the others soon followed, falling down to the deck in obvious fear.

"You lead," one of the pirates said. "We'll do whatever you want."

Whatever she wanted. That was a long way from what they'd been threatening only a minute or two ago. A part of Ceres wanted to punish these men for what they were, and what they did, but she pushed down that urge. She wasn't going to do that, even if they did deserve it.

Besides, her ship was ruined.

"Take me to Delos."

CHAPTER ELEVEN

Thanos had decided not to attend the Stade for the Blood Moon festival. The sight of the Killings would only have brought back too many memories of Ceres, and that wouldn't have been fair to Stephania. A man should concentrate on his wife, not on the dead.

Besides, there was too much of a chance that Lucious would be there, and after this morning, Thanos wanted to avoid his half-brother even more than usual.

That was why he was in the castle when the guards started rushing about. Thanos knew fighting men. He knew the difference between the speed that came with a hurried order from a superior and a genuine emergency. One look at the guards rushing to get their weapons in order, looking around as though not knowing what to do, told him which this was.

"What is it?" Thanos asked, stopping one of them. The man had the look of a city guard, not one of the castle contingent. His uniform was less pristine, and there wasn't the flash of a royal insignia at his shoulder. "Calm down. Tell me what's happening."

"Prince Thanos." The man sounded breathless, as though he'd run all the way from the city. "Thank the gods you're here. We've been trying to find someone senior to take charge, but Prince Lucious isn't here, and in the wake of the Blood Moon festivities…"

All the others who might have done so were probably too hung over to be useful, Thanos thought. He'd sent away the two generals who'd been there.

"You've found me now," Thanos said. "What's the emergency?"

"It's the Stade, your highness," the guard said. "The rebellion has attacked the Stade!"

A flicker of interest and hope flared in Thanos, but he did his best to disguise it.

"What do you mean, soldier?"

"In the middle of the Killings, your highness," the guard said. "They attacked the Stade and freed the combatlords. Now… now the whole area around the Stade is rioting! They're in open rebellion, and we don't know what to do!"

Inwardly, Thanos cheered in joy at the audacity of the move. It was brilliant, in its way, striking at the heart of the Empire while acquiring truly dangerous fighters for the rebellion. The rioting around the rest… handled properly, it might turn into full rebellion in the city.

He'd just been handed the opportunity to do it.

"Right," he said. "From this moment, I'm in command. What's your name?"

"Gil, your highness."

"Well, Gil, you're with me. I hope you know how to ride."

Thanos raced for the stables, saddling his horse as quickly as he could and ordering the stable hands to fetch one for the soldier while he grabbed his weapons. Together, they rode down into the city, and it probably looked to the guard as though Thanos was hurrying to try to put down the rebellion. Instead, Thanos wanted to get there so that he could see it for himself and look for ways to fan the flames.

There were *real* flames as the two of them rode down into the city. People had set fires in some of the poorest areas, and Thanos could see smoke rising in curls while guards, looters, and rioters fought on the streets.

"Noble scum!" A man ran at Thanos, a knife in his hand. Thanos kicked him away and kept riding.

"You don't want to stop and finish him, your highness?" Gil asked. "Prince Lucious would—"

"There's no time," Thanos said, cutting him off. It wasn't the real reason, but it was one a guard might believe. "Where are the officers currently in charge?"

"We're not sure *who's* in charge, your highness, but a few of the officers have found a spot in one of the old towers overlooking the Stade."

"Then that's where we need to go," Thanos said, spurring his horse forward. The streets were closing in now, and in the side streets, he could see groups of people gathering. Most of them looked as though they were just standing around, as though they wanted to know what was going on.

If he'd had more time, Thanos might have gone to them and urged them to revolt with the others. As it was, he rode in the direction of the Stade, and even from here, he could see the signs of violence. There were groups of guards in the streets, and even as he watched, a cluster of them set off after a running man.

"Leave him!" Thanos ordered. "I need you with me."

He and his group of guards advanced through the streets. In one, he saw a group of what were clearly looters smashing their way into houses. He saw them dragging a man and a woman from one. It was obvious that they intended to rob them, and probably murder them, taking advantage of the call to rebellion to steal or settle some old score.

"With me!" Thanos said and charged forward. He drew a sword and struck out, making a man fall back as he clutched a bloodied stump of an arm. He parried a blow from a club, then kicked another man back. The guards were there then, fighting off the others and setting them to flight.

"Are you all right?" Thanos called down to the man and woman who had been dragged from their home.

"I—" the man began, "they were going to kill us. Thank you."

Thanos pointed to the guards accompanying him. If he had them to command, he should at least use them in a way that protected the people of the city. "These men will stay here and make sure that they don't come back. Stay inside. It will pass soon."

Except that Thanos was hoping it wouldn't. He was hoping it would turn into something more as he set off toward the Stade again. Far more.

The Stade was ahead, and so were the old towers. They were so ancient they had probably been there as long as the city, reaching up in pure white marble so high that they almost rivaled the castle's bastions or the spires of some of the city's temples. Normally, they were empty, but now Thanos could see the guards standing around the base, obviously unsure what to do next.

Inside, there was a spiral staircase running around the wall of the tower, leading up to a level far above. Thanos ran, ignoring the burning in his muscles as he made it to the top level. There, he found half a dozen men in the uniforms of guard captains, soldiers and royal guards, all arguing and shuffling orders.

"And I say that we need to move now, Maximus," one said. "Without waiting for orders."

"And risk angering the king, Pullo?" another countered.

Thanos decided to take charge. "What move were you thinking of making?"

The men there stared at him. The one called Pullo bowed low.

"Prince Thanos. We hadn't expected that *you* would come."

"I hadn't expected to be here," Thanos said. From the top of the tower, there was a good view out over the Stade and the rest of the city. From there, he could see the violence in the Stade, and it was chaos.

There were fights in every corner of it. Thanos could see knots of guards in the colors of the city, engaged in outright battle with rebels, with combatlords, or simply with people in the stands. The combatlords were easy to make out even from up here, standing proud in the chaos, whirling and leaping, killing almost effortlessly. There were fires in the Stade too, burning in the stands where people had set light to whatever they could.

"Look at them," Maximus said. "Animals."

Thanos shook his head. "Just desperate people. How bad is it?"

"There are riots in the Stade and all the surrounding streets," Maximus explained. "We have lost—"

"Temporarily," another of the soldiers interjected.

"We have temporarily lost control of half of the lower district next to it."

Thanos tried to think. Could this be turned into the loss of the entire city? Could this be the moment when things changed in the Empire? Below, the violence certainly felt as though it might never cease. There were guards down there, but too few to ever fully contain the chaos. Thanos felt as though he was floating above it up here, but even so, the violence felt almost close enough to touch. In a nearby street, he could see men and women ripping up the cobblestones with their hands, flinging them in the direction of an advancing group of guards.

"What are you doing to regain control?" Thanos asked. "*Can* you regain control, or do I need to evacuate my wife from the castle?"

His throat tightened at that thought. He wanted the rebels to succeed, but he also knew the kind of violence that could accompany a revolution. He would not allow Stephania to be caught up in that. He needed to find ways to help the rebels, but if they were already winning, he would ride back to make sure that Stephania and any other innocents in the castle got out of the city safely. He'd already seen what the mob in the city could be like.

"There should be no need for that, your highness," Pullo said. "We have more than a thousand good soldiers in place outside the city gates, ready to advance at your command."

"Our thought was to advance and surround the Stade," Maximus said. Thanos could practically hear his need for royal approval. "We can trap the rebels and the combatlords in there, then tighten the ring like a noose. We can attack them from all sides and end this. Maybe we can even capture some of the leaders of the rebellion."

Thanos had to admit that it was a good plan. It was simple, but there was a kind of strength in that. There was nothing to go wrong, only a constant kind of pressure that would crush the rebels under the weight of numbers.

Thanos had to find a way to stop it.

"No," he said. "We can't do that."

"Why not?" Maximus demanded, then seemed to realize what he was saying. "Forgive me, your highness. I don't mean to speak out of turn, but I'm not sure you understand everything that might be at stake."

Thanos tried to think, and one hard, harsh truth rose up in him like bile: this wasn't going to be the moment when the rebellion overthrew the Empire, or even the city. There were too many soldiers waiting. Even if this thousand didn't put down the revolt, there would be more to follow.

All he could do now was try to salvage some kind of victory for the rebels, even though the thought of what he would have to do was pure pain. He had to choose, right now, which lives to spare and which to take.

"It's you who don't understand what's at stake," Thanos said, trying to put as much authority into his tone as possible. "Do you think the Stade matters at this point?"

"Your highness," Pullo said, "that's where the rebels *are*."

"There are rebels in every corner of the city," Thanos snapped back. "You, Gil, didn't we have to fight a group of them on the way here?"

"Well, I suppose so," the guard who'd brought him said.

Thanos went on before anyone else could argue or contradict. He changed his tone to that of a general giving a speech before a battle.

"The truth is that the rebels are in the city. There are fires spreading, and riots growing in every district. A thousand men sounds like a lot, but it will barely be enough to control the whole city. I want the soldiers divided up, with city guards running each group. I want patrols on every major street. I want the fires controlled, and any looting stopped. We go out and we show the people that we control every street. Where there are rebels, we engage them, but the priority is showing that the city belongs to us."

Maximus still looked skeptical. "What about the Stade?"

"We put in a cordon around the Stade," Thanos said. "Two hundred men."

"Two hundred? That—"

"You will do as I have ordered," Thanos said. Two hundred was far too few to stop the rebels slipping out. There would be holes in the line. There would be escape routes. "I will not take the Stade while hordes of rebels march on the castle to kill my family and my wife! We will hold the city until the battle in the Stade burns out, and then we will move in to take what's left."

And in the meantime, soldiers would be putting down the revolt everywhere else. It would have happened anyway, but now that Thanos had given the order, everything the soldiers did would be down to him. Every death, every beating, would be because he had given this order. Here at the top of the tower, he wouldn't see the executions, but he would know they were happening.

He just had to hope that the rebels in the Stade would make it.

CHAPTER TWELVE

Lucious wandered through the aftermath of the revolt in the city while the soldiers swept away rioters. No one challenged him. They knew who he was, and the men around him were hard men, tough men, whom it was better not to ask questions of.

It wasn't the same as his raids had been, though, because the guards were being far too restrained by comparison. No gibbets, no whippings in the street. Hardly even any executions. It was almost as if they didn't want to clamp down on the city where their friends and families lived. He made a mental note to look into bringing in mercenaries from the further corners of the Empire. Men who wouldn't hold back.

On another day, he would have ensured it happened in Delos. He and his men would have gone on a binge of violence through the city, paying back the rioters and the rebels for daring to rise up. On another day, he would have been the one there when they wanted a commander for their forces, rather than his brother, Thanos.

His brother. Just the thought of that made Lucious curl his lip in anger. He was the heir. Delos was *his*, whatever the books said.

"Just down this way, your highness," Vrek said.

Lucious had brought a quartet of guards with him, replacements for the ones he'd lost to Thanos. Vrek was a former bandit, who had joined the army because it offered better pickings. Quellon and Fen were both equally massive. They looked like they might be brothers, although that was hardly a thought to calm Lucious right then. Justino was whip thin and good with knives.

"You're sure this is where the people I want will meet?"

The former bandit shrugged. "This is Delos. These kinds of people aren't hard to find."

The tavern was a long way from anywhere Lucious would normally have chosen to drink, even on one of his forays into the city with the other young nobles. There were places that held the dashing hint of danger, and then there were places like this.

It was stone built, but probably only because the patrons would have burnt down anything wooden. The doors were iron bound and the windows had bars, making the place look more like a fortress than just a place to drink. Instead of a sign, a ram's skull hung above the door. From inside, Lucious could hear the sounds of people drinking and yelling to one another, shut in while the rest of the city fought.

"I'd have thought that people in a place like this would be out looting," Lucious said.

"Begging your pardon, your highness," Vrek said, "but looting is a mug's game at a time like this, and people in here will know it. Stuff you could steal any day of the week, with a whole army's worth of soldiers out to kill you if they so much as see you outside."

Lucious shrugged off the familiarity for now. "I don't need a lecture on the finer points of reaving etiquette. Just get me *inside*."

It took his men perhaps a dozen blows before the door's lock broke open. Lucious stepped into a room that had long since fallen silent. Rough-looking men stood frozen, halfway to standing, obviously caught off guard by the sight of their prince entering the room. Many of them wore cloaks, their features hidden under the cowls. Lucious found himself wondering if they'd done that when his men started pounding on the door, or if they actually drank there like that. He strode over to the tavern's bar and put down a coin, spinning it so that the gold gleamed in the sunlight.

"Wine," Lucious said, "and this will pay for the door."

The barkeep snatched up the coin as Lucious let go of it, coming back with a skein of wine. Lucious held it, but didn't drink it. Behind him, he heard the sound of men settling back into their seats. He didn't look round. These peasants wouldn't dare to attack him.

"I'm looking for information," Lucious said. He took out another coin and spun it. "My men told me that this might be the right place to come."

"Maybe your men didn't hear right," a voice from the back called out.

Lucious turned and nodded. Vrek and Justino moved forward and dragged out one of the cloaked figures while the two brothers watched the rest. Some looked like animals tensed to spring, but they didn't. Perhaps they could guess what would happen if they attacked the heir to the throne.

Lucious stood and pulled the cowl from the man's head. He had probably been a strong man once, but now the years were taking their toll.

"My men hear very well," Lucious said. He struck out, catching the man in the stomach with his fist, hard enough to knock the breath from him. "Mostly because they know when to be quiet and listen."

Lucious went and sat down again. He went back to spinning his coin.

"I've seen things," he said to the room. "I want to know what they mean, and that means asking you. Believe me, I wouldn't be here if I didn't have to be."

Given the choice, he would have burned this place down with everyone there still in it, but sometimes it was necessary to do unpleasant things like associating with this scum.

"I saw Prince Thanos this morning," Lucious said.

"Most of us did," another of the tavern's patrons said. "He was the one putting down the riots."

"Before that," Lucious said, pushing down his anger for the moment. "I saw him riding back toward the castle early this morning. He's been sneaking about. I want to know why."

"Then why not ask him instead of interrupting our drinking?" another of the men there asked.

Lucious sighed and drew his sword, laying it down on the bar. He looked over to his men. "You see what happens?" he asked. "I try to be reasonable, and people just throw it back in my face."

He sprang forward, snatching up his blade and swinging it in one motion. Blood sprang from the inn patron's throat as Lucious cleaved through it. He died as easily as any other peasant. Strange; Lucious had expected more.

Now the other patrons reacted, and for a moment Lucious felt real fear. They sprang up from their seats, knives and clubs clearing their sheaths. His men moved into formation around him, and just for a second, Lucious thought that maybe he'd miscalculated. Then he remembered who he was.

"Harm me, and you'll watch your families flayed before they finally impale you," Lucious said. He drew a pouch from behind his back. "On the other hand, if you help me, it could be very profitable for you all."

He threw it into the blood on the table, and the clink of it cut through the silence. Slowly, Lucious felt the tension in the room dissipate.

"Never did like Eskrin much anyway," one man muttered, and that seemed to be the cue for the others to sit down again, even if they kept their weapons on the tables.

"Always did have a big mouth on him," another agreed.

The first man shrugged. "Not a problem anymore."

Lucious went back to his seat. Now, he *did* sip the wine. He needed it after how close that had been. It was vile stuff, watered and sour from being left out too long.

"Thanos," he said, letting the words sit. "I want to know anything you've heard about him. I want to know why he's sneaking about. And don't tell me that you haven't heard anything. There's always something. There had better be, anyway, if you want the soldiers to give this sty a miss."

The men there looked at one another before looking at one of their number in a corner, a small man nursing a glass in both hands. Lucious saw him swallow as the eyes turned to him, and when Lucious nodded, his men brought him out.

"Your friends seem to think you know something," Lucious said. "Now, as you may have noticed, I don't have a great deal of patience, so I'd advise you to say what it is."

The man stood there, opening and closing his mouth. To Lucious, he looked like a fish.

"Justino here is quite good at getting information from people, I hear," Lucious said. "He can do things with knives that—"

"There are rumors," the man said.

"There are always rumors," Lucious said.

"These are about Haylon."

That was enough to catch Lucious's interest. Absently, he wiped the blood from his still wet sword blade.

"What's your name?" Lucious asked.

"Alexander, your highness."

"Well, Alexander, what about Haylon?"

"I… I don't know much," the man admitted. "I just… know people who know people. People who claim to be in the rebellion. People who've been to Haylon. I've only heard a few things."

"And what are they?" Lucious asked as he put his sword away.

"Just that things weren't as they seemed there with the first expedition," Alexander said. "That the story Prince Thanos told about it wasn't the real one."

"So what is the truth?" Lucious asked.

"I don't know," Alexander admitted. Lucious saw him pale. "But I… I could find out. I know the right people."

Lucious smiled slowly. Today was proving more interesting than he'd expected. "Then I think you should ask them, don't you?"

"Y-yes, your highness."

Lucious saw him squirm in place. "What is it?"

"It's just… the people I'll have to ask… it's not the sort of information that comes cheap."

Lucious took another pouch from his belt, flinging it down alongside the first.

"Consider that a down payment," he said. He looked around the room. "No. Consider it a retainer, for all of you. From this moment forward, you're my men." He held up a hand as some of those there started to mutter. "I know, I know, you're all busy with your own little 'business enterprises.' I have no interest in interfering with that. If you want to steal or kill or sell the weak, that's your business. *My* business is the truth about Thanos. Help me with my business, and you'll find it easier to go about *your* business."

"You're offering us protection?" one of the patrons asked.

Lucious gestured to the thugs he'd brought with him. "I look after my men," he said. "Ask them if you like. Ask how good the pickings are, and how much freedom there is to do what they like. So long as you also do what *I* like, you'll never have to worry about the guards again."

"And there will be gold?" one of the others asked. "You're still offering us gold, right?"

"I'm offering you a choice," Lucious countered. "I'll pay you for what you do. If you need to bribe informants, or buy secrets, I'll pay. If you give me information, I'll pay. If you give me enough to have Thanos's head... I'll give you your weight in gold. Of course, you could choose to ignore all that. You could try to walk away, or to cross me."

He walked over and drew his finger through the blood of the man he'd killed. Peasant blood, but he'd gotten used to the feel of it.

"If a man chooses that, he becomes my enemy. I'll hunt him down. You'll all get coin for any betrayers you find for me. Then... well, there are torturers in the castle who can keep a man alive for weeks if they want. Long enough to see everyone he loves executed, at least."

Lucious wiped his hand on the dead patron's tunic.

"But it's your choice, of course. I wouldn't want to pressure you. Now, if you'll all excuse me, I'm going to enjoy the Blood Moon while there's still some of the festivities left."

He walked from the tavern, his men falling in behind him. Lucious didn't have to wait to know what decision these peasants would make. He would go back to the castle, and soon enough, one of these men would deliver Thanos to him. Thanos would die, Stephania would be begging at his feet to be his, and the world would be as it should be.

CHAPTER THIRTEEN

Ceres stood at the prow of the pirate ship as it bore down on a harbor village far to the north of Delos, and her heart filled with the sight of home. The village wasn't a large one. It had a natural harbor, wooden buildings clustered around a central square, and fish dried in the sun on racks, prior to smoking.

Tears came to her eyes. After all these moons, she would be home at last. She thought of her family, of the rebels, of the destiny awaiting her—and her heart quickened.

On the shore, she could see people running around in response to the approaching ship. This close, she could hear the tolling of an alarm bell, and she could see guards in the uniforms of the Empire forming up, ready for battle. At least a few people were riding clear on horseback, and Ceres couldn't help a moment of regret at that. She didn't want to scare them, but the pirate ship was the best way for her to reach the mainland again.

Ceres saw a spiked chain rise from the water, lifted across the harbor by the villagers. Obviously, they'd had to deal with pirates before. She felt the stilling of the ship's rhythm as the oarsmen struggled to bring it to a halt, caught up on the chain.

"This is as far as we can go," one of the pirates told her, and Ceres could hear the note of fear then. He didn't even suggest being allowed to raid the village.

"Then I'll make my own way to shore," Ceres replied. "You have small boats?"

"Two, my lady."

"Then any man you've taken for the oars who wishes to leave is to be allowed to do so."

"But we can't sail the ship at full speed if—"

"It will move a lot slower if it's stone," Ceres replied, her tone hardening as she cut him off. Life on the boat was hard. The only way to keep respect was to show no weakness. "Now do it."

While she waited for them to obey, she went through the ship, taking what she needed. There was no armor that would really fit her there, but she managed scraps and fragments of it, piecing them together in a way that felt vaguely reminiscent of the Stade. She still had the stone dagger Eoin had given her on the forest folk's island, but to it, Ceres added one of the curved swords of the pirates, and a pair of etched steel bracers that ended in gauntlets of metal scales.

"When I'm gone," Ceres said, "put back out to sea. If you've any sense, you'll stop robbing people. I've spared you once, but if I catch you again…"

She let that hang while she watched the boat go down into the water with more than a dozen men aboard. Ceres could have gone with it, but she could see an easier way to the shore. With the lightness and balance the islanders had taught her, she walked her way along the chain the villagers had raised, hopping lightly onto the shore.

She watched the contingent of Empire soldiers as she approached. There were probably twenty of them, arranged in a square. They stood as if not knowing what to do. They'd probably been expecting to have to deal with a boat's worth of pirates, not one woman. Ceres walked up to them as calmly as she could.

"Halt!" the leader of the soldiers called. "Who are you? What are you doing here?"

"I don't want trouble," Ceres said. "I'm just passing through here."

"And those pirates just happened to give you a ride?" the officer demanded. Ceres saw a soldier beside him touch his shoulder. "What is it, Rikard?"

"Sir, it's her, sir!"

"Who?"

"Ceres! The rebel! I saw her at the Stade when I was south in the city, carrying messages."

"You're sure? I thought she was dead."

Ceres drew her blades, holding them out to either side, feeling the weight of them. She could have lied about who she was, but the Empire needed to understand what was coming for it.

"I'm not dead," she said. "And you should run."

"Run?" the officer said. "There's twenty of us! No one can beat twenty armed men. Not the greatest combatlord who ever lived. Certainly not some girl who played at it. So here's what's going to happen. You're going to surrender or we'll beat you senseless. Then we'll take you in chains down to the city."

"Not to Lord West?" the soldier who'd spoken before asked.

"Lord West?" the officer countered. "The man's halfway to being a rebel himself. The only reason he doesn't join the rebellion is because he's worried about losing his lands. No, we'll take this one where she belongs. Grab her."

The soldiers broke ranks as they started forward, and that was when Ceres attacked. Their officer had been right. The greatest combatlord couldn't have fought twenty men. They would have been rushed and brought down in seconds, but she was more than just a combatlord. She had the training of the forest folk. She had the power that came from the Ancient Ones' blood. Put together, it was as though her attackers were corn waiting for the scythe. The only reason she didn't turn them all to stone was because she suspected the effort of it would be too much for her.

She cut down one with a sweep of her curved blade, stepped through the line of men and stabbed out at another with her dagger. She spun and kicked, smashing away a soldier who tried to grab her and continuing to move.

A club came at Ceres's head. She ducked underneath it and answered with a sword stroke, then parried another attack with her bracers, ripping a weapon from its wielder's hand. She leapt, clearing the heads of two men who tried to tackle her, landing lightly.

She kept moving, because stillness was the one thing that could bring her down now. There were still enough soldiers to simply pile in and bring her down in a scrum of flailing limbs, so Ceres didn't give them the chance. She was so much faster than they were, so much stronger, that it was easy to keep the soldiers in one another's way. She stepped out of the way of another rush, stabbed one man with her dagger, and slammed another soldier into the frame of a door hard enough to crack it.

The strangest part about it wasn't the speed or strength with which she moved. She'd experienced that before in the Stade, in flashes. The part that went beyond it was the way it felt like a part of her now. It felt natural. Indeed, the whole fight felt like some bloody dance in which Ceres already knew the steps. She'd been opened up to the power within her, but she'd learned more than that. She'd learned to fit in with the world around her. She opened herself up to the battle, and let it tell her exactly where she needed to move.

Ceres swayed back from a slash, parried a thrust, and countered with a blow that took an Empire soldier in the leg. She spun and she struck, her blades always moving, always intercepting or striking, shoving away or cutting through. She felt the warmth of breath behind her, and was already ducking as a soldier moved in to grab her. Ceres sent him sprawling into the dirt.

The moments blended. There were so many swords around her, so many attackers, and yet Ceres didn't feel the fear that she should have at it. Instead, she felt almost serene. There was something beautiful about the act of moving with a blade in her hand, even if the consequences of it were so terrible.

Her bracers caught the sun, shining as they deflected blades, reflecting the uniforms of men as her fists slammed into them. The soldiers got in one another's way as Ceres kept moving, never still for long, never pausing to let them regain the formation they'd given up.

Maybe if they'd managed to circle her, and strike at her from all sides, they might have had a chance. Maybe if they'd been more than just ordinary soldiers, barely trained and used to peasants who didn't fight back, they'd have been able to slip past the whirling circle of her blades.

As it was, man after man attacked, and then fell. They started to push to keep out of Ceres's way, to not be the one to have to fight her next. Ceres felt as though she was pushing through trees in a forest, except that these were trees lined with blades, any one of which could still hurt her or kill her.

Suddenly, Ceres found herself in clear space, facing off against the officer who'd ordered her taken. She could tell just from the way he stood that he'd had more training with a blade than most of his men. Certainly, the sword he held was finely worked, honed to a razor's edge.

He thrust and Ceres parried, keeping her distance. She had to keep moving, because there were still other men around her. None seemed to be attacking now, and Ceres guessed that they were hoping their officer would deal with her where they couldn't, but she still couldn't afford to let her guard down. She moved around the officer, continuing to parry.

"You might be able to best these scum, but I was first sword in my unit, back in Delos. They used to give me criminals still armed, when they wanted it to look as though they'd died fighting."

Ceres didn't reply. Instead, she continued to circle. She tried a cut, and the riposte was fast enough that she was grateful for the speed her power gave her. She leaned away, pushing aside the thrust, but it seemed to embolden the officer.

"Look at you," he said, striking and striking again. "You're not so dangerous. You're nothing. Probably only got into the Stade because you were trying to seduce—"

Ceres struck while he was still mid-sentence. The officer's sword came up to parry, and she rolled her wrist around it, her blade cleaving down through his armor from shoulder to mid-chest. She let go of the hilt and let him fall, already looking for the next threat.

There wasn't one. Half a dozen soldiers were running by now, but that was all that was left of them. The rest lay in a broad circle around her, dead, unconscious, or simply wounded too badly to run.

The adrenaline of the fight passed in a rush, and Ceres stood shaking as the scale of what she'd done hit her. Fourteen men. She'd cut down fourteen men. Men who would have happily killed her, but that did nothing to clean away the blood from the village square around her, or from her armor. She'd cut them down easily, thanks to her training, and her powers.

It had felt as natural as breathing. Now, Ceres had to remind herself to do that, catching the iron tang of the blood in the air while she stood and waited for her heart to return to normal.

Ceres could see the people looking out from their houses, as though wondering what she was. Ceres had an answer to that at least. She was of the blood of the Ancient Ones. On the island with her mother, she'd started to get a sense of what that meant. Now, with so many people staring at her over the bodies of the dead, she felt as though she'd learned another side of it.

She heard the sound of hooves over the silence of the square. She looked up to see horses approaching; so many that it seemed like half an army. Easily a hundred men, all armored in mail, all carrying long spears for throwing or jabbing down with at full charge. Ceres doubted that even she could survive if they attacked.

One had a pennant attached to his lance, marked with a stylized weather vane, being blown by the west wind. He rode forward from the mass of them, stopping short of her and raising the visor of a helm in the shape of a boar's head. The face beneath was surprisingly young.

"What happened here?" he demanded. Ceres could hear the note of fear there.

"They attacked me," she said, as if it explained all of it. In a way it did.

"And you killed that many men?" He sounded as though he couldn't believe it. Ceres didn't blame him. She could barely believe it herself. Even now, the violent beauty of it seemed like some kind of dream. Some kind of nightmare, but she couldn't let them see that. She had to be more than just a girl standing in a square then. She had to be a symbol.

She stood as openly as she could, trying to wear the blood that covered her more like a badge than it felt.

"I fought in the Stade. I was cast out by the Empire. I survived their prison ships. And yes, I killed that many men, but only because I will not let the Empire control my life any longer."

"I must bring you to Lord West, ruler of these lands, and allow him to decide your fate."

He squinted into the light.

"What is your name?" he asked, as if beginning to recognize her.

"I am Ceres," she said proudly.

A gasp erupted from the crowd.

"That is not possible," he said. "Ceres is dead."

For the first time, she allowed herself to grin.

"Not anymore."

CHAPTER FOURTEEN

Thanos stood in the king's council chambers while around him, the senior nobles of the Empire stood and applauded. He clutched a scrap of paper deep in his fist, clinging to it while the noise rang around him. At the head of the great oval table, his father sat impassively next to Queen Athena, but Thanos searched his face. Even now, even hating all that this man represented, he wanted to find some hint of pride there.

At the back of the room, he could see Lucious watching. Lucious wasn't applauding with the others. Instead, his expression was intense, following every movement Thanos made.

"Well done, Prince Thanos," the master of the king's forests said. "Without you, we would be having our throats cut by rebels even now!"

"I think the royal guards would have handled it," the captain of the royal bodyguard replied.

The master of coin shrugged. "I'm grateful that we don't have to find out."

King Claudius stood. "Enough of this. I want to know what happened today. How did things get so out of hand? Naymir, you're meant to have control of the Stade."

Thanos saw a sweating nobleman take a small step back.

"Who would have thought that rebels would attack *there*, your majesty?" the man said.

"No one here, apparently," Queen Athena said with obvious disdain. "And as a result, how many were harmed in the Stade?"

"We don't have full numbers yet," Thanos said. "We don't know how many people were killed on the on the Stade floor, and as for the streets around it—"

"How many *nobles*?" Queen Athena said, cutting in. "Who cares about a few dead peasants?"

"Perhaps if we'd cared more," Thanos pointed out, "it wouldn't have come to this."

"Oh, poor Thanos," Lucious said. "Still with a heart bleeding for the peasantry."

Thanos might have argued, but the captain of the royal guard chose that moment to speak.

"There were perhaps a dozen minor nobles at the Killings, your majesty," he said. "Four were killed, two suffered injuries serious enough to require the healers, and the others escaped with cuts and bruises."

"Were they anybody important?" King Claudius demanded. "No? Then we have more important things to consider. Like how this happened. I thought we were crushing the rebellion, piece by piece."

If he thought that, Thanos thought, then he really didn't understand how these things worked. He created more rebels with every act of cruelty. The Empire was like a drowning man who needed to swim but instead only thrashed.

"I have been attacking rebels wherever we can find them," Lucious said. "Applying pressure to force them into submission. Eventually, we will crush them."

Thanos saw King Claudius shake his head.

"I don't care about 'eventually.' I care about what happened at the Stade. Thanos, you're here to report, so report."

Thanos gripped the paper in his hand tighter at the casual way his father treated him. As though he were just some officer to be commanded.

"The commanders down by the Stade sent a runner as I was returning from a morning ride," Thanos said.

"You're fond of those," Lucious muttered in the background. Thanos ignored him.

"He reported that there was violence around the Stade, and that no one was available to take control of the situation." Now he did allow himself a pointed look in Lucious's direction. "He'd been trying to find Lucious, but he wasn't there."

"Enough squabbling," the king said. "Why was the runner not able to find one of my generals? General Olliant might have left for Haylon, but Haven should have been around."

Thanos looked around, hoping that no one caught his look while he tried to see if anyone was suspicious.

"The old fool has probably wandered off," Queen Athena said. "He's well past his usefulness. Honestly, husband, can you imagine the mess he would have made of this?"

"Possibly," King Claudius said, but he looked thoughtful. "Go on, Thanos. What about when you got to the Stade?"

"The captains there reported on the situation," Thanos said. "And I saw that the biggest risk was of the situation spreading beyond the Stade. I deployed troops to the streets to ensure that didn't happen."

King Claudius steepled his fingers. "I have spoken to the captains, Thanos. They said that they urged you to surround the Stade and move in to take it. Is that true?"

73

"It is," Thanos said, because there was no way he could deny it. "They didn't grasp the full situation."

"As far as I can see," Queen Athena put in, "the situation was that you had a chance to capture the leaders of the rebellion, and you failed to take it. You do know that they escaped?"

"I know," Thanos said. He tried to fill his voice with regret. He wasn't made for this, for politics and secrecy, but he had to do it. "I also know what would have happened if rebels had reached the castle."

"From what I hear," Lucious said, "the real rebels weren't in the streets. That was just a rabble."

"You weren't there!" Thanos snarled back, grateful that Lucious made it so easy to be angry. "I was. I heard that there was violence on the streets. I *fought* rioters, and I had to make a choice. I had to choose between crushing the Stade and risking that coming here. Here, where my wife was still in our bed. Where all of you were. Where *you* Lucious, were presumably still sleeping off the festivities!"

"And if I hadn't, do you think the rebels would still be free? I don't take things so gently."

"You might think I made the wrong choice out there," Thanos replied, "but that's the point. I was the one who was there to make the choice, and I made the one that would keep my family safe." The nobles there probably thought that he just meant Stephania. The king and Lucious would probably be wondering. "I won't be questioned on that."

He turned and made for the door. No one stopped him, which was probably as well. He was running out of answers. He'd bought some time by making his actions look like an emotional outburst, but there would still be questions.

He didn't have time to answer questions, because of the scrap of paper in his hand. It had come by raven this morning. Just six words.

The sculpture garden. Noon. Meet me- A.

***

The sculpture garden was an ode in stone to Thanos's ancestors, yet he couldn't feel comfortable there. Carved images of kings since the start of the Empire stared down, along with their wives, children, generals, and favorites. The first king, Ullian, sat atop a rearing marble horse, the broken granite body of a creature that could only have come from the depths of the artist's

74

imagination beneath the hooves. After all this time, the marble features atop the horse were weathered to the point where Thanos couldn't make them out. Would he have seen a resemblance there if they hadn't been?

"The Great King Ullian, crushing the Ancient Ones," Akila said, stepping from behind another statue. The rebel leader looked a little more battle worn than he had back on Haylon, but he was still spare-framed and dark-haired, with a short beard and a tinge of dark humor in his expression. As always, he wore two short stabbing swords at his waist.

"It probably didn't happen like that," Thanos said. "Cosmas, the royal scholar, is always saying history is more complicated than you think."

"No? It's the story I heard. The founders of the mighty Empire, freeing humanity from the yoke of the Ancient Ones, bringing fair and just rule to all." That brought with it one of the sardonic smiles that the rebel leader seemed to specialize in. "Of course, for an Empire supposedly founded on rebellion, you and your family seem remarkably resistant to it now."

"I'm surprised to see you here," Thanos said. "I wouldn't have thought you could leave the rebellion just to talk to me."

"I needed to see if another story was true," Akila said. He didn't draw either of his swords, but his hands rested on the hilts.

"Akila?" Thanos said with a frown. "What's going on?"

"You tell me," the rebel leader snapped back. Thanos saw him take a step forward. "I let you go because of how much you helped us on Haylon. You swore brotherhood to us."

Thanos didn't give ground. "And I've been working to help you. I sent you a warning of the attack on Haylon."

"An attack they're saying you ordered," Akila snapped back, and now one of his swords did clear its sheath. "We captured soldiers and they were talking about how you rode down to the docks to appoint the general attacking us."

"Because he's incompetent!" Thanos retorted. He took a step back now, and found himself pressed against the statue of Ullian, literally depending on his ancestors for support. "I only found out the morning that they sent the fleet. I had to forge orders to stop it from being commanded by one of our greatest generals."

"Our greatest generals?" Akila said. He moved forward, his sword pressing to Thanos's throat. Thanos shoved the other man away.

"You know what I mean," Thanos said. He didn't draw his own blade, but he wasn't just going to let Akila murder him. "You know I'm on your side."

"Do I?" Akila demanded. "This general of yours is a long way from incompetent. He's plodding, but plodding is dangerous when you have the men. Now, I hear that you commanded a force that put down a rebellion here."

Thanos shook his head. "I was trying to ensure that it succeeded."

"By sending troops into the city?"

"The troops were coming anyway!" Thanos insisted. "All I could do was ensure that the leaders of the rebellion had enough time to get away."

He saw Akila stalk among the statues. The rebel leader lashed out, hacking a chip out of a marble figure's arm.

"You have all the answers, don't you?"

"If I had *all* the answers, I would have found a way to bring down the Empire by now," Thanos said.

"Would you?" Akila asked. "You'd bring down the nobility, and all the cruelty that goes with it? Then why did you marry one of them?"

Thanos thought of Stephania, and of all the joy he'd had with her. He wouldn't let even Akila make him feel bad about loving her.

"You wouldn't understand," Thanos said. "Stephania and I are happy together."

"So why should I believe that you want to disrupt all of that?" Akila demanded. "You know why I came here? Why I took a boat in the middle of defending my home? Because if anyone was going to kill you for betraying us, I swore it was going to be me. I was going to look you in the eye, and if you'd betrayed us, I was going to do the job myself."

There was a time, after Ceres's death, when Thanos might have let him do it. Now, though, there was too much to fight for. Too much still to do.

"I haven't betrayed you," Thanos said. He could feel Akila's gaze on him. "You told me to come here and do this, when I wanted to fight."

"I think you actually believe that," Akila said. "You really believe you're doing what we want. If you hadn't sent that warning, you'd be dead by now. As it is… I don't know what to make of you, and I don't have enough time to waste working it out. Thanks to you, I have an island to defend from a plodding general who has seen every trick before. Thanks to you, the rebellion here has been set back by who knows how much. I'm not going to kill you, Thanos, but you aren't one of us either, not really."

"I'm risking everything for you," Thanos said.

"We're *all* risking everything," Akila replied. "But some of us do it in ways that don't involve marrying nobles and having rebels butchered." He shook his head. "I have to get back. Thank you for your warning, but if this is your idea of helping, we can do without it."

Thanos watched him walk back among the statues, quickly disappearing among the still marble figures. He couldn't believe that Akila had come. More than that, he couldn't believe that Akila didn't trust him, after all he'd done.

He would find a way to do more. He had to.

CHAPTER FIFTEEN

Stephania walked the grounds of the castle, searching for her husband and taking a moment to enjoy the sunlight. Down in the courtyard, where servants and soldiers bustled about their duties, the world seemed brighter today, and had ever since she'd learned the news at the feast.

It was still hard to believe that she was really pregnant, but just the thought of the tiny life growing inside her filled her with joy. She hadn't told anyone, and it was far too early for the pregnancy to show, but right then she wanted to shout the news to the world.

Not until she'd told Thanos though. So far, Stephania hadn't even told her maids for certain. She wanted Thanos to be the first to hear the news, and to learn about the child they would be bringing into the world.

Stephania allowed herself a moment to daydream about what it would be like. Thanos, she had no doubt, would be a wonderful father, doting on his son or daughter, kind and protective, loving and strong. Stephania would need to ensure that their child got the core of ruthless steel that would see them through the world, but Thanos would be the one to try to ensure they never needed it.

Stephania loved him for that, and for so much else besides. Soon, their lives would be as close to perfect as Stephania could imagine.

She was drawn from her reverie by the sight of a man making his way across the castle's courtyard. He was grubby, dressed in the uniform of a soldier, but looking nothing like the pristine guards of the castle. Stephania wouldn't have given him a second look, might even have called for the guards to remove him, except that she recognized him.

"Fikirk, what are you doing here?"

The man looked around, and yes, it was definitely him. The same harried look, as though constantly expecting to be attacked. The same collection of scars, collected more in barroom brawls than in the wars he claimed. He was the kind of man Stephania would normally never admit to knowing, but he'd been a useful informant over the years, providing information from within the armies of the Empire that most of its generals could only wish for.

She normally communicated with him at second- or third-hand, or occasionally by meeting in secluded spots. She certainly hadn't summoned him to the castle today.

"My lady," he said, with an attempt at courtly manners that was frankly embarrassing. "I hadn't expected to see you today."

"If you hadn't expected that, then what are you doing here, Fikirk?" Stephania shook her head. It had to be important, whatever it was. The man wouldn't have come if it weren't crucial, and she wasn't about to let the man get away without telling her. "Come with me."

"My lady..." Fikirk said with a glance around. He was obviously looking for a way out.

"Do you want me to be seen out here with you?" Stephania demanded. "More to the point, do you want to continue receiving the stipend I send your way?"

She saw the man swallow, but he went with her. She led the way to a small side chamber. Not one of her own rooms, of course. That would have created too much of a chance of being seen. Instead, she picked a room that was probably used for storage, filled with sacks and crates that had probably been taken from peasants' homes.

She carefully propped the door shut so that no servant would dare to interfere, then returned her attention to the informant.

"Do you understand the difficulty you've created for me by coming here unannounced?" Stephania demanded. "If people see you here meeting with me, then they'll know that you're one of my informants."

"Maybe they'll think I'm a lover," Fikirk joked, and just the thought of it was enough to make Stephania feel ill. Or maybe that was just the pregnancy. "That was the story they told about old Xanthos. Haven't seen him in a while. Was he really in your bed?"

The way he said that made Stephania pause. Her informants weren't supposed to know about one another. They certainly weren't meant to know about the people who arranged more dangerous matters for her, or to make guesses about what had befallen one who had become too dangerous.

"Wouldn't you like to know?" Stephania countered with a forced laugh.

"Oh, are you shocked that I know about him?" Fikirk asked. He tapped his nose. "I work things out, I do. Wouldn't be much use otherwise, would I?"

"I think you'd better prove yourself *very* useful right now," Stephania said. "You obviously came here to tell me something."

To her surprise, Fikirk looked down at his boots like some naughty child caught out stealing sweetbreads.

"Not to see... *you*... as such, my lady."

Stephania sighed. She should have guessed that this would happen. That was the problem with informants. They had no sense of loyalty.

"Who then?" Stephania demanded.

"Well, you see, it's tricky—"

"You'd best make it a lot less so quickly, if you want to continue working for me," Stephania said.

The soldier took a look around the storeroom and spat. Stephania saw a rat scurry away across the floor. It seemed that even his own sort wanted nothing to do with Fikirk.

"Well, I guess I have been working for you for a while," Fikirk said, "but Prince Lucious wasn't exactly what you'd call subtle in his recruiting strategy, you know?"

"Lucious? You're here to see *Lucious*?" Stephania asked.

"Not exactly," Fikirk said.

"His people, his thugs, whatever he wants to call them," Stephania said, waving that away. The point was that her informants were working for a man she'd assumed to be too arrogant and stupid to employ any at all. Lucious was the kind of man who assumed he knew everything anyway, so why would he employ informants now?

"Well, it was Prince Lucious who set me off looking, but what I found..." Stephania waited out Fikirk's pause. "I think I might go straight to the king with this. Isn't as though Lucious will pay me what he says."

"And what does he say he'll pay?" Stephania asked, taking out a small pouch of gold. "Maybe I can outbid him?"

The soldier shrugged. "It would take more than that. This information is worth a man's weight in gold."

"And maybe you'll get that from the king," Stephania said, "but this is what I have now. Think of it as me paying for a preview."

Even with that, the man seemed reluctant. Was he really that ungrateful after all the time he'd spent working for her?

"I don't know, Lady Stephania. You might not like what I have to hear."

"All the more reason for me to hear it then," Stephania snapped. Why was she spending all this time in a dank storeroom? Only some sense that this was truly important kept her pushing. She had gotten where she was today by never letting things happen without her knowledge. She drummed her fingers on the edge of a crate, then decided to try a different approach.

"You aren't thinking this through, Fikirk. You've come here because you don't trust Lucious to pay you. Maybe the king won't either. You're already a part of his army."

"I have the proof stashed," Fikirk said. "Well, more or less."

"And you think that will matter?" Stephania countered. "Tell me now, and you can still try to get what you can, but you'll at least have something for the information."

"Hmm…"

Stephania knew she had him with that small sound. It was just a matter of waiting.

"All right," he said at last. "But like I said, you won't like it. You're going to have to work out what to do about your husband. Prince Thanos is a traitor."

Maybe he put it that bluntly because he wanted to see the look of shocked disbelief rise up to overtake Stephania's features. She could already feel her mind racing, grasping for any explanation, any straw.

"No," she said. "He's a prince of the Empire!"

"And he's working with the rebels," Fikirk insisted.

Stephania shook her head so hard she thought it might fall off.

"Oh, not those here," she heard Fikirk say, and it seemed as though it was coming from a distance. "Didn't you ever wonder what happened to him on Haylon?"

Of course she had. She'd wondered, because somehow her attempt at revenge had gone wrong.

"Fishermen found him," Stephania said.

"Rebels found him," Fikirk insisted. "Ever wonder why Thanos was one of the lucky ones? They took him in as a prisoner, and he helped them to beat Draco's men. Then today, I heard he helped replace Olliant with old Haven for the new expedition."

It couldn't be true. It had to be some lie, made up to discredit Thanos. Except… Stephania had seen him fight Lucious to protect the common folk. She knew he'd argued with the king, and she'd heard the rumors about what had happened in the Stade. That he'd had a chance to crush the rebels and hadn't. She'd assumed that it was just Thanos not wanting to risk the people of the city, but what if it was more?

"Is that all of it?" Stephania asked.

"It's enough, I reckon," Fikirk said.

It was. It was enough that Thanos would find himself branded a traitor, regardless of who he was. And that would mean only one thing, because the king didn't allow rebellion. Thanos would die.

"No," Stephania whispered to herself. "No."

Stephania tried to compose herself, but she couldn't stop the feelings welling up inside her. She was so used to being in control. She planned things well in advance, but there was no way to plan around this. How could she not have known all this about Thanos? How could she have been so stupid, not to learn it earlier?

Why didn't it make a difference to her?

She should have been planning then. She should have been thinking about ways to extricate herself from this, maybe even about bringing the information forward herself. But she couldn't. Not when it was the father of her child. Not when it was Thanos.

"Well, that's all I know," Fikirk said. "So I guess it's time to pay me so we can see how the king likes it."

Thanos was a traitor. Stephania knew it, deep in her bones, but the truth was, she didn't care. She didn't care if she had to kill half the Empire to keep him safe, either. The only thing that mattered was that he was hers, and nothing, *nothing* was going to destroy that.

"Yes," Stephania said, hefting the bag of gold. She threw it, lobbing it high and to the right of the soldier. He had to reach out wide to grab it, half turning to snatch it out of the air with a grin.

That was when Stephania stabbed him.

She hadn't planned it. She'd never stabbed anyone herself. Poison was so much neater. So much cleaner. But she didn't have time for poison, or even to think. All she had was the small knife that she kept for eating, like everyone else. It barely seemed like enough to kill someone with.

It still slid up under Fikirk's ribs easily enough, jabbing upward toward the heart as his blood spattered. Stephania pulled back in disgust at the wet heat of that, trying to wipe herself clean while the guard staggered, trying to grab his own blade. He fell to his knees, and Stephania simply stared at him.

"You can't... stop this," he managed, and Stephania stepped in to stab him again, then again. She didn't stop until she was certain he was dead on the floor in an expanding red pool.

CHAPTER SIXTEEN

Ceres stared up at Lord West's fortress home with a deep sense of foreboding. She had agreed to come along on the ride, willing to at least hear what this lord had to say before, if need be, fighting to the death. After all, she was back in her homeland now, and nothing, no lord, would stop her.

Lord West's castle was craggy and gray, with a keep sitting on a hill above a larger enclosure, only the presence of flowers growing around the walls offsetting the forbidding look of it.

She rode closer on a horse one of Lord West's men had loaned her. The creature was pale and skittish, so that Ceres spent as much time comforting the horse as looking at the castle around her. Even so, she could see the difference between this and the castle at the heart of Delos. That was a place designed to terrify the local populace into submission. This had more of a strong, protective feel to it. There were plenty of ordinary people living within the protective outer walls, in slate cottages that made the lower section seem like a village in its own right.

She had heard much of Lord West over the years and had heard, as far as nobles went, he was a fair one. But she still wasn't taking any chances. She eyed all possible exits in case she had to fight her way out of there, to the death, and flee on foot or on horseback.

The horsemen around her dismounted, and Ceres walked with them up the slope to the central keep. At least they gave her the respect of not trying to detain her. She went through the large entrance gate, following the warriors' leader through into a hall dominated by long tables. The warriors spread out around them, taking places that looked as though they were long established.

Another table sat at the front, and at it, Ceres saw a man in his forties working on documents with the aid of a pair of clerks.

"If the Empire's men have burned the fields, then I'm not going to expect them to provide grain, but my men still need to be fed. For the winter, give them work helping in the weavers' workshops while they replant. We can trade the extra for spelt from the hill farms."

"Yes, Lord West."

He looked up, and Ceres stared right back at him.

Ceres saw a man with shaggy, graying hair, a neatly trimmed beard, and deep brown eyes that seemed to take in everything about

83

her at a glance. His clothes were finely made, but they were not the silks and fripperies of Delos's court, and they looked well worn.

"Gerant," he said, with the faint burr of a North Coast accent, "I sent you out because the riders from the Empire's contingent said there was a threat of pirates landing in the village, yet you seem to have brought back a single young woman with you. Please explain."

"She was what I found when I got there, uncle," the young man who'd led the warriors said. "A few other men alighted from the pirate ship, but they were clearly freed slaves. This was the only armed person there."

"If she's a pirate, hang her," Lord West said. "You know I won't allow any harm to befall my people."

"She isn't a pirate," the young man, Gerant, said.

"Then what is she?"

Ceres took a step forward. "Why don't you ask me that yourself?"

She heard a faint intake of breath from the soldiers around her as Lord West stood up and walked down to her. He was taller than she was, with the slightly bulky frame of a once strong man who now spent too much time indoors.

"I am Lord West of the North Coast," he said. "My family was given these lands as stewards in the days when the Ancient Ones still walked. My line is longer than that of the current king. Who exactly are you, young lady?"

"I'm Ceres," she said, trying to match the confidence in the nobleman's voice. "I fought in the Stade. I joined the rebellion. The Empire tried to kill me and failed."

Ceres thought she saw Lord West blink at that.

"When I heard who she was," Gerant said, "I thought you would want to speak with her, uncle."

"Do we have evidence that she is who she claims to be?" Lord West asked, never taking his eyes from Ceres.

"When I found her in the village," Gerant said. "I found her surrounded by the bodies of Empire soldiers. She'd fought twenty of them and won."

"Twenty men?" Lord West said. "That isn't possible."

Ceres made herself shrug as if it were nothing. "It's possible for me. There's a reason I fought in the Stade, and I've learned a lot since then."

She watched the older man's face.

"If you are who you say you are," he said at last, "then by the loyalty I have sworn to the Empire, I should put you in chains."

84

There was something about the way he said it that made it into a question. A man like this would know that Ceres must have come to his home for a reason, and now he was asking why.

"You owe them no loyalty," Ceres said. "When I came in here, you were talking about them burning your fields and killing your people. You're obviously a man who cares about those he rules."

"Enough to avoid getting them into wars they cannot win," Lord West said. "Yes, I have seen the things the Empire has done, but that does not mean I must throw away my people trying to change it all."

"If you don't, who will?" Ceres insisted. "It's easy to sit back and look after your little corner of the world, but if everyone does that, when will things ever get better? The Empire is stronger than any one of us, but it is not stronger than *all* of us."

"Ah, so you want us to join your rebellion," Lord West said. "You want me to join with people who would probably gladly see me thrown off my lands, my family and friends cast out."

"It isn't about that," Ceres said. "It's about overthrowing a tyrant, not overturning the world. You must have seen the things that are done in the Empire's name. If you put your own interests ahead of stopping it, then they're being done in your name as well." She had a question she wanted to ask. "Why do your men not wear the uniforms of the Empire's army?"

"Because then they would have to take the orders of the Empire's generals, even if that means burning villages," Gerant said beside Ceres. "My uncle would never allow that."

"But he can speak for himself," Lord West said. "My nephew has made some of the same arguments to me. But there is another reason why my men wear my colors. It is to show that they are *my* men. That we are not the Empire. That we exist to protect the people, not to command them. But by the same token, we will not come just because someone else calls."

"Then protect your people," Ceres said. "I have traveled to places and seen things that I never thought I would see, but all the time, I was thinking about the way things were back in the Empire. I was thinking about everything it has taken from me: my brother, my family, the man I loved—"

Thoughts of Thanos still brought the ache of loss with them. For all the things Ceres had learned, she hadn't found a way to shut that pain away. She shook her head.

"Again and again, the Empire has hurt me," she said. "It put me in the Stade to die, and I didn't. It put me on a ship to the Isle of

85

Prisoners, and I survived. But how many more are not surviving? How many people die every day because we do nothing to stop it?"

"Many," Lord West said. For a moment, a note of sympathy crept into his voice. "And I can understand why you have every reason to hate the Empire. I have more than a few reasons of my own."

For a moment, Ceres thought that she had him.

"Then act on those reasons," she said. "Lend me your men."

"However, the fact remains that my family swore to serve the Empire, and I will not be the man to betray that. Honor matters. Loyalty matters. No, I'm sorry," he said. "Unless you can give me a better reason, I will be forced to take you prisoner. I have no choice."

"And hand me over to the Empire?" Ceres said.

She saw Lord West shake his head. "You will remain here. I can do that much, but no more."

"The Empire did not give your family its lands," Ceres pointed out. "The Ancient Ones did."

She heard a small sound of annoyance from Lord West. "And if you can produce one of them to command me, I will obey. Until then, though, you are merely wasting both of our time. Gerant, please escort the young lady to the north tower and secure it."

Ceres stood, summoning the power that lay within her. Before in the Stade, she'd managed to pull a weapon into Thanos's hand. Now, she reached out for the sword at Gerant's belt, wrapping her power around it and pulling with it. She wasn't sure it would work, but she wouldn't turn the men around her to stone. They weren't pirates or soldiers of the Empire, and they'd been nothing but courteous to her. She reached out with her power...

...and a second later, she was holding the sword belonging to Lord West's nephew.

Ceres heard men rising to their feet in a rush of armor, the scrape of blades clearing sheaths filling the hall. She knew she had to act fast, because if she didn't take advantage of this moment, she was simply someone who'd ended up holding a weapon in front of their lord.

"I don't need to produce one of the Ancient Ones," Ceres said, "because I *am* one."

She saw Lord West hold up a hand to halt his men. He stood there, staring at Ceres as though he couldn't quite believe what he'd seen.

"You're truly one of them?" he asked at last, in a tone so filled with awe it hardly seemed like the same man.

She held out the sword, closed her eyes, and wrapped her fingers around the blade. She felt them turn to ice, and felt the power flowing through her.

She opened her eyes and saw the sword in her hand turned to stone.

More than that, she saw the horrified looks of the warriors all around her, looks of fear, which slowly morphed to awe.

Lord West, most of all.

She dropped the sword, and the stone shattered, skidding across the floor in pieces. One stopped at Lord West's boot.

Lord West stood there for several more seconds. Then, using the table for support, he did the one thing Ceres hadn't expected.

He knelt.

"We are sworn to serve the Ancient Ones," he said. "All of us."

One by one, the other warriors followed his lead and knelt.

Ceres surveyed the room. She took a deep breath, feeling her destiny manifest within her. She had seen this moment, in a dream or in some other dimension, she could not be sure.

"The time has come to undo some of the evil the Empire has been bringing with it. Will you lend me your soldiers, Lord West?"

"There is nothing to lend," Lord West replied. "If you are one of the Ancient Ones, then they are yours by right. I will send messengers to all who owe me fealty, and they will send whatever soldiers they have."

Ceres reached out a hand, helping the older man to his feet. She turned back to the room.

"You've already heard what I have to say," she said. "I want to take you south, all of you. I want to join up with the rebellion, and fight against the tyrant who has oppressed all of us for far too long. Lord West says that you will go with me, but I know it is him you owe your loyalty to, not me. So I will not command you to go with me. I will simply ask it. Will you travel with me? Will you strike at the heart of the Empire, and overthrow the king who has your lands burned and your people killed? Will you fight?"

At first, Ceres thought she hadn't persuaded them. She'd been expecting some great cheer. Instead, she got silence, but it was a silence that came to be filled with a dull thudding that grew piece by piece. She realized that it was the sound of the men banging their sword hilts on the table, the rhythm of it filling the hall.

And she knew that war was on its way.

CHAPTER SEVENTEEN

Thanos crept his way along tunnels by flickering candlelight, wheeling along a box on a two-wheeled trolley more normally used for transporting sacks of grain. The squeak of the wheels was the only sound he could hear down there. The candle stub he held gave off a firefly glow of orange, illuminating walls to either side, close enough that he could have reached out and touched them both.

It hadn't been easy to find this place. Just to keep slipping from the palace was getting harder, because Thanos had to do it in a way that Stephania wouldn't notice, and Lucious seemed to be taking far too much of an interest in his movements too. Doing it with the box he wheeled had been even harder.

Then he'd had to bribe people in some of the poorest parts of the city, and that hadn't been easy when his face was so well known. He'd had to come down into the slums wrapped up in an old cloak, being careful never to let anyone glimpse his features.

The entrance had been at the back of a butcher's yard, behind sides of beef and pork hanging on hooks. Thanos had felt the eyes on him as he descended into the depths of the tunnels beneath the city, and seen the cleavers close to the hands of the men there. He had a sword and dagger under his cloak, but he'd come without armor. He wasn't there to fight.

He kept wheeling his box down the tunnels, and now, Thanos thought he could hear sounds ahead. There was the clang of hammers, and a faint feel of greater heat, mixed in with a deep orange glow that might have come from fires somewhere nearby.

The tunnel he was in opened out a little, and there was the sense again of eyes watching him as he made his way through the tunnel system. Thanos didn't know if he was going the right way, but he could at least follow the sounds of the hammering and hope that it led him to what he was looking for.

The rebellion.

Akila's words had stung. Thanos had thought of the man as a friend, as something close to a brother. Yet the rebels on Haylon didn't believe that he was doing all he could, and Thanos could understand why. So he was going to do more, and if the rebels on Haylon wouldn't take his help, he would do it for those in Delos instead.

Thanos found an opening in the tunnel he was walking along, which gave way to a room where hammering seemed to dominate everything else. Thanos saw men and women hammering away on anvils and working metal in forges. The sound, heat, and rhythm of it were almost overwhelming.

When it stopped, the silence was worse.

"Who's that?"

"I don't know him."

"What's he doing here?"

Thanos saw the smiths and workers grabbing for hammers or recently finished weapons, hefting them as they tried to decide if they should be attacking him or not. Thanos looked around and saw men coming into the cavern behind him, armed with a variety of weapons that could only have come from the Stade. He saw a woman with them, thin and tough looking, but more than that, he saw the way they looked to her as though waiting for orders.

He threw back the hood of his cloak, hoping that this wouldn't be the last thing he ever did.

"I know him," a man called, and Thanos recognized a combatlord when he saw one. "It's Prince Thanos!"

"A royal? Kill him!"

Thanos saw several of them start forward, and braced himself for what was to come. He couldn't hope to fight all of them, even if he wanted to.

To his astonishment, a young man, still just a boy, really, stepped in front of them all. To his even greater surprise, they stopped.

"You're right," he said, "that's Thanos, which means he does more for the people around Delos than any other royal. It means my sister, Ceres, loved him. We shouldn't kill him."

"Your sister?" Thanos said. "That means you must be Sartes."

The boy nodded. "Come on, all of you. If you were a combatlord, you've trained with him. You know what he's like."

Thanos heard a murmur of assent go around the room.

Sartes went on. "It isn't *Lucious* standing there."

"Maybe it's worse," the woman from the doorway said, and Thanos could hear the authority in her voice. "Lucious is an evil thug who doesn't know any better, but it wasn't Lucious leading the attack on Haylon. It wasn't Lucious who put down the riots in the street a few days ago. It wasn't Lucious who sent General Olliant looking for us, or who got Ceres killed because she loved him!"

The last point seemed almost to make her angrier than the rest of it. Thanos guessed that she'd been close to Ceres, whoever she was. Even so, he couldn't keep himself from snapping back.

"And I loved her!"

"We should at least hear him out," he heard Sartes say. "Please, Anka."

Thanos had heard that name. The mysterious head of Delos's rebellion. The woman who had replaced Rexus. Strange, he'd been expecting someone... different. Older, stronger, more dangerous looking. Maybe she'd found herself having to grow into a role she hadn't expected, the same way he had when he'd learned who he was.

"You think I was behind the attack on Haylon?" Thanos said. "I joined the rebels there. I helped them to fight off the attack. Since I got back, I've been looking for information to pass on to them. I warned them of the new attack, and I even switched the generals so that Olliant wouldn't be descending on the island with a massive army."

"Instead, you sent him looking for us," Anka said.

"You killed him?" Thanos asked.

"We have him," Anka said.

Thanos nodded. "Good. That was the idea."

He saw the rebel leader cock her head to the side. "It's easy to say that now."

"Just as it's easy to say that I'm the one who allowed you all to escape the Stade," Thanos said. "It doesn't make it any less true."

He heard another murmur go around the room. He saw one of the former combatlords there thump his chest.

"Allowed us to break out, boy? We *fought* for the freedom we had. There were hundreds of the Empire's men there."

"Two hundred," Thanos agreed. "Two hundred men holding a cordon around the Stade, when there should have been a thousand closing in on it. I sent the others to hold the city, because it was the best move I could make to give you all a chance."

"Do you have any proof of that, either?" Anka asked.

"You're still here," Thanos pointed out. "You heard about the troops in the city. Ask questions, and you'll soon find out what the captains wanted to do."

To Thanos, Anka looked thoughtful. He could see her looking around the room as though trying to guess at the feelings of the others there.

"Why would I have come alone?" Thanos asked. "If I could find this place, then I could have brought troops with me. I could have filled this place with soldiers, but I'm here alone for a reason."

Thanos saw an older man step out of the crowd. He was wearing a blacksmith's apron, but he wasn't carrying a hammer or a weapon right then. Instead, he walked over to Thanos, holding out a

90

hand for him to take. Thanos grasped it, feeling the strength there and seeing the assessing look in the other man's eyes.

"I'm Berin, Ceres's father. They say my daughter loved you," he said.

Thanos met his gaze. "More than you could ever know. If I hadn't been sent to Haylon—"

He saw the other man nod. "If I hadn't gone looking for work. Or if I hadn't left her in the Stade while I tried to free my son. There are a lot of ifs in this world. You married a princess quickly enough after my daughter died, though."

There was a challenge in that. Thanos could hear the question the older man was really asking: had he truly loved his daughter, if he'd been able to move on so soon?

"Stephania helped me through it when I was… broken," Thanos said. "It was as though my heart had been ripped out of me, and she found a way to fill that hole. She was the woman I was always supposed to marry, but that doesn't mean I don't think about Ceres every day."

"We both do," Berin said, pulling him into a bone-crushing hug.

That seemed to be enough for Anka. "All right. I believe you." She raised her voice. "No one is to hurt Thanos. It seems that we owe him a lot. But there's still the question of what you're doing here, Prince Thanos."

"I'm here to help you," Thanos said as Berin pulled back from him. That got some looks of surprise from around the cavern, in spite of all that he'd just said. "A… friend told me that I should be doing more than I am."

"What did you have in mind?" Anka asked.

Thanos looked around the underground forge. "I can see that you're trying to produce weapons and armor, but what if I had a way for you to take enough to supply an army?"

"Unless you're planning to help us raid the royal armories…" Anka began, and she obviously caught Thanos's expression. "You are, aren't you?"

"Not the castle," Thanos said, "but the army has staging posts and warehouses where weapons and armor are gathered together before they're sent out to the army."

"They do that in secret," Anka said. "And never in the same place twice. But that doesn't matter, does it?"

Thanos shook his head. "I know where. The next shipment will be going out from a warehouse on the north side of the city, supposedly used for bolts of cloth. There will be guards, but not many, and disguised as private thugs because their best defense is secrecy."

"So that's what you're here to bring us?" a woman toward the back asked. "A tip that might just as easily be a trap?"

"That's enough, Hannah," Anka said. "This could be a huge moment for the rebellion."

"We need more than just weapons," the woman continued. "We have the combatlords, but we need more people. We need resources."

A young man in richer clothes than the others nodded. "We need to be able to hire tradesmen and soldiers," he said. "My father's money will only go so far. We need to be able to spread the rebellion to every corner of the Empire, and even with the most audacious raids, we can't do that one move at a time."

"Trust you to be thinking about money, Yeralt," said a man who seemed to be armed mostly with knives.

"The world runs on money, Oreth," the other man countered. "The Empire continues because no one has the resources to stop it."

"It continues because we don't work together to fight it," Thanos said. "But you're right, gold matters. Which is why I brought this."

He kicked over the box that he'd brought, letting the lid fall open and the contents spill out onto the floor. Coins glinted gold in the forge light, while the gems amongst them seemed to have an inner fire of their own.

"They won't miss this from the royal treasury," Thanos said. "Or, if they do, they'll assume it went to the army."

He saw Anka smile at that. "We're going to fight the Empire using its own gold?"

"You're going to do more than fight," Thanos said. "You're going to win."

He'd taken a risk, getting the gold like this, but it would be worth it if the rebels could make use of it to support their cause. With this much gold, they could hire mercenaries, or they could buy horses. They could acquire ships or find more smiths. They could buy food, supplies, whatever they needed.

With this much gold, the rebellion could build an army.

She stepped forward and clasped his arm, and slowly, she grinned.

CHAPTER EIGHTEEN

Lucious stalked into the throne room with bad grace, barely looking round at the empty spaces where there would normally have been assembled ranks of nobles forming phalanxes to either side and leaving a clear path to the thrones his mother and father occupied. When he stopped before the dais, his bow was perfunctory at best.

He had better things to do than be there.

"Ah, Lucious," King Claudius said. "I trust we didn't drag you away from anything important?"

His tone said quite clearly that he doubted it. Probably, he thought that Lucious had been busy drinking or hunting, sleeping or running down the peasantry. Even his own father didn't take him as seriously as he should.

"I came as quickly as I could," Lucious replied.

In fact, he'd spent days working his way through reports and rumors, half truths and untruths. He'd listened to idiots droning on about things they'd heard, or thought they'd heard when it came to Thanos, only to find that they'd been making it up as they went in the hope of getting gold out of him. His only consolation had been the things he'd been able to do with them in the dungeons after they'd disappointed him.

"I'm sure you did," his mother said. "We have important news."

Lucious wondered if he should tell her what a dangerous profession that was at the moment. Curiously, he hadn't been the only one getting rid of informants. In the last few days, it seemed that there had been almost a quiet epidemic of deaths, by poison, by stabbing, by apparent accident. It looked almost as if someone was trying to deprive Lucious of the use of his newly acquired network.

And now that it seemed there might finally be some answers from it, he found himself summoned here, in front of the court, to stand uncomfortably amidst the Great Hall and wait for his father to declare whatever it was this time. So long as he didn't actually recognize Thanos, Lucious didn't care. Although Thanos didn't seem to be here today, which suggested something else entirely.

"What is it you require, your majesties?" Lucious asked. Well, he couldn't just tell them to get on with it, could he? "If you want me to crush the rebellion more thoroughly, I will need more men, and permission to—"

He saw his father wave that away. "Forget that. We have bigger concerns than simply taking more from ungrateful commoners."

There was something about his tone that made Lucious pause. "What is it?"

It was his mother who answered. "We have reports in from the north. Birds came today from one of our garrisons on the edge of Lord West's lands. There is an army heading south, towards Delos."

An army? Lucious couldn't keep the shock off his face. The Empire did not get attacked by armies, not this close to home. It had to deal with small forces of rebels, or threats on its farthest borders. It didn't have to worry about armies advancing on its greatest city.

"Lord West is leading an army?" Lucious said. He shook his head. "I don't believe it. The old fool is loyal. He'd cut his own head off if you commanded it."

"The army contains Lord West's men, but he is not the one leading it," the king said. "He and all the old lords of the North Coast have joined under a different general."

"Who?" Lucious asked.

"Ceres."

Lucious could feel the blood draining from his skin, although whether it was in anger or fear, he couldn't say. Both seemed to be competing for top position within him, swirling round and round without any resolution.

"What? I thought she was dead!"

His father held up a hand before he could go on to rail at the unfairness of it all. "We all did, and for now, it will remain a secret that she has survived at all. It would disturb the people to hear it."

"The people, or Thanos?" Lucious asked.

He saw a flash of annoyance cross his father's face. "Do not go against me on this. Do you want to risk the commoners rising in revolt?"

"They wouldn't dare."

"Wouldn't they?" Queen Athena asked. "If they heard that a girl we built into a symbol of the rebellion so we could kill her is back, that she *isn't* dead... it would be a powerful blow to us, my son."

Perhaps they would rise up after all. Lucious had to admit that he had no idea how the lower orders thought.

"We want no one to hear of her return, least of all Thanos, until we are able to say for certain that she is dead again," King Claudius said.

"And where do I fit into this?" Lucious asked.

94

The king smiled. "You're going to lead the army to deal with her."

Now fear won out over the anger. Lucious didn't mind dealing with unruly peasants, but Lord West commanded a powerful collection of horsemen, and Ceres... His mind went back to the times she'd beaten him far too readily.

"Me?" Lucious said. "Don't we have generals for this sort of thing?"

"Apparently not," King Claudius said. "Olliant is still busy on Haylon, although we haven't heard much from him. Who knows where Haven is? I will not put the army under Thanos, for obvious reasons."

Like the part where he would probably rush into Ceres's arms in the middle of a battle. Even so, Lucious found himself scrambling for alternatives. The sensible thing to do in a situation like this was not for the heir to the throne to go out to meet the enemy in open battle. It was for him to sit nice and safe behind thick walls while others undertook the dangerous work.

"Surely we can recall one of the generals?" Lucious said. "Or if not them, what if—"

"You will lead this force, Lucious," the king said, and suddenly there was steel in his voice. "You've been happy enough to lead when it just involved butchering rebels. Well, these are also rebels, and they must be dealt with."

"But Father—"

"No," King Claudius said. "No more arguments. You will do this. I keep giving you chances to show that you are a man, Lucious. You ran away in the Stade. You shy away from real work. You must show the people of the Empire, show *me*, what a great king you could someday be! That means crushing this army yourself, not leaving it to someone else. People respect strength, so it is time for you to show some."

Lucious looked to his mother, his jaw already growing tight with the need to say something, but there was no help to be found there.

"You will make us proud, Lucious," she said.

Lucious mostly felt like running away, but he couldn't say that. Instead, he gave a stiff bow.

"As you command, your majesties."

"The closest legions of the army have been gathered outside the city," the king said. "They will expect you there with them by sundown. Do not disappoint me, Lucious."

95

There was something about the way he looked at Lucious that said Lucious already had. That said he would much rather Thanos were the one standing there. Maybe that was the point of this. Maybe his father secretly hoped that Lucious fell in battle, so that the king could say that actually, there was another heir. Or that he ran, so that he could be disinherited. Lucious wouldn't put it past him.

Well, Lucious would do it. He would go, and he would crush the army, and he would bring Ceres back impaled on a spear for all to see. Before that, though, he had business to attend to. Business that would hopefully ensure Thanos was never a threat again.

***

The upper rooms of the Ram's Skull tavern were, if anything, worse than the one beneath. Lucious looked around with disgust at the splintered floorboards, the soiled bedclothes, and the mold growing from the walls. There was a door on the far side, connecting to another room that would no doubt be even worse. If he could have risked meeting somewhere better, he would have, but there had been no time. As it was, he and his bodyguards had been forced to race across the city to get here.

The man they were there to meet was hardly much better than the room. To Lucious, he looked like the kind of beggar who might have occupied any street corner in Delos: straggle-bearded and wild-eyed, filthy and rag covered.

"You said you had information?" Lucious said. "I find it hard to believe a man like you has information about anything but bedbugs."

"Mad Fal sees a lot of things," the beggar said. "He finds things."

"I bet you see things," Lucious said. "Probably after drinking too much."

"Mostly because people think I'm stupid," the beggar said, his voice changing and suddenly sounding as though he could have been from any of the richer sections of the city. "But I've found what you're looking for."

"And that is?" Lucious asked.

The beggar pushed open the door to the adjoining room. In it, a man sat who had burns down one side of his body, his beard giving way to the scar tissue where the two crossed. He wore the clothes of a sailor or a porter, but on the stand beside the bed, Lucious saw the flash of the Empire's insignia.

96

"This is Todol. He was on Haylon."

"You were one of the soldiers in the attack?" Lucious asked.

The man looked up as though only just realizing that Lucious was there. His look was so blank that Lucious might have thought he was some kind of empty shell, but he nodded.

"Todol doesn't say much," the beggar said. "Not after the fire on his ship. But Mad Fal, he knows how to get him talking, he does."

The beggar gave the bearded man a drink. Lucious could probably also think of a few other ways, depending on how well this went.

"And what does he have to say?" Lucious asked. He turned to the man. "What did you *see*?"

The man's mouth cracked open. "Thanos. Prince Thanos betrayed us."

They were the words Lucious had been hoping to hear. "Go on."

"He went over to the rebels. He led them onto our ships. He shot burning oil at the shore, then he fired our ships so we couldn't get around the rebels. I was on one. I only survived because I threw myself overboard. Others did too, but the sharks—"

"Yes, yes," Lucious said, with a hint of impatience. "I'm sure it was terrible. But you survived."

"Barely. The rebels hunted us down one by one. I thought it was just because they hated us, but no. It was so we couldn't tell stories of the spy they'd sent back. So we couldn't say what Prince Thanos really was. I got back by hiding on a boat and then killing the crew."

"But you didn't come forward before this?" Lucious demanded. "I might almost think that you're only saying this because I'm offering the reward."

He saw the man gesture to his scars. "Do you think I did *this* for the reward? I tried to say nothing. I tried to hide and stay safe. Now, it seems like they're killing anyone who knows. I told a man I used to be in the army with. He went to the palace and didn't come back. I need a way to stay safe."

"I can provide that," Lucious promised. He would have promised anything right then for the information he needed. "Just tell me all of it. And quickly."

He sat, and he listened. He didn't even have to feign interest. When the former sailor was done, Lucious smiled to himself.

"If you repeat this when I tell you to, you'll be a rich man."

"And me?" Fal the beggar asked.

"You'll be paid, don't worry."

The beggar nodded at that. "Then I have some other information you might like too."

Lucious raised an eyebrow. "All of this, and there's more?"

"As I said, Mad Fal sees things. You know Lady Stephania pays the informers?"

"I know that," Lucious said.

"Well, would you like to know *everything* she's done?"

Lucious thought, but only for a moment. He put an arm around the beggar, even managing not to wince while he did it.

"Why yes, Fal. I think I would."

CHAPTER NINETEEN

Ceres sat high in the saddle of her horse as they rode south toward Delos, grateful that the horse was a fine one. Otherwise, she would never have managed to keep up with the riders of the North Coast around her. They rode in a horde of shining mail shirts and gleaming spear tips, banners rising over their horse backs to proclaim the subdivisions of their houses. Lord West and his nephew rode beneath their weathervane banner, but Ceres knew that it was *her* they were following. She just hoped that she could live up to their expectations.

The moment she'd revealed her Ancient One ancestry, it had been as though she'd been in some kind of dream, because things had happened so smoothly. Lord West had sent out messages, and riders had come in response almost too quickly for Ceres to believe. She didn't know if they had come from hatred for the Empire, loyalty to the lord of the North Coast, or some distant memory of the times when the Ancient Ones had ruled, but they had come in the hundreds.

Then thousands. More than two thousand horsemen now rode at Ceres's back. An army, and one to be feared thanks to the easy way they sat in the saddle. Some were minor nobles or the sons of old families. Some were their retainers or soldiers who had wanted a better path than joining the Empire's main army. All were well armed and steel armored. Some had spears, others hunting bows they could fire from the saddle. Ceres had already seen them do it, bringing down rabbits or birds to cook at their campfires.

"We will be at Delos soon, my lady," Lord West said, riding close to Ceres. It was strange to hear the note of deference in his voice. The older man treated her the way Ceres saw others treat him: with deference and a sense that of course she would know the correct thing to do. He'd rejected any suggestion that he should stay behind, and now sat wearing mail armor reinforced with plates that he didn't look entirely comfortable with. Even so, he sat comfortably in the saddle, and if his swords sat uncomfortably on his hip, Ceres still had no doubt that he knew how to use them.

Ceres tried to look as confident as he felt. That was one of the strange parts of this. She was as much a symbol as a leader, and she couldn't afford to show any weakness. She kept riding, keeping pace with the others along forest trails and across open ground. Her horse never seemed to tire, keeping going so that its strides seemed to eat up the ground in front of her.

She and the others rode up a rise, and at the top, Ceres raised her hand to bring the army behind her to a halt. Delos lay ahead in the distance.

How long had it been now since she'd been there? Weeks, at least, possibly longer. So much had changed that it seemed like a lifetime ago. She hadn't seen her family since her father had sneaked in to visit her in Delos's castle. They probably didn't even know if she was alive now, and the thought of that made her feel sick, but she had no idea how best to contact them.

"Tell the men to get whatever rest they can," Ceres said, while she looked down at the city.

Lord West nodded. "I'll have them make camp."

Delos didn't shine, except around its castle. There were too many slums, too many areas of the city that were barely scraping by, for that. With the wind blowing toward them, Ceres could already make out the stink of the city, of too many people crammed into too small a space. She could see the Stade there, and the castle, the walls that looked like those of a prison holding in the inhabitants.

And she could see the trenches set out on the plain before the city, too.

There was an army there, the uniforms of the Empire a bloody red in the sun. Its men were spread out before the city, obviously there to intercept Ceres's advancing army. The trenches looked freshly dug, broad and lined with spikes, obviously designed to stop horses.

Ceres sat there looking down at it, watching the way the soldiers moved. She was no expert on battle tactics, but she could see the way the Empire's army was laid out. The trenches were designed to stop horses, or at least slow them down. Meanwhile, the strongest soldiers would probably be on the edges of the line, there to swing around and crush any force coming into the middle.

If her army did what it was designed to do and charged, it would be carnage. If they could persuade the Empire's forces to move ahead and try to attack, it would work far better, but Ceres couldn't imagine them giving up their position like that. What was left? A long, drawn-out game of archery and hitting at the edges? No, because Ceres suspected other Empire forces would be marching this way.

So, what did that leave? Ceres looked down again at the forces below. She could see a figure in golden armor leading them, shining like a beacon among a horde of officers, hangers-on, and toadies.

Even at this distance, she recognized Lucious.

A part of Ceres wanted to charge down regardless of the trenches, just leap across them and cut Lucious down for all he'd done. If she killed him, though, it wouldn't make things better. It would only remove one fragment of the Empire's evil, not change things completely.

What if it could though? An idea came to Ceres, one that might get them around the trenches and the armies. That might solve this directly, *and* give her the revenge she wanted when it came to Lucious.

"Lord West," she said. "Can you fetch a flag of truce?"

"Truce, my lady?"

"Don't worry, I didn't ride all this way to give up," Ceres assured him. "But I *do* want to talk to them."

In the end, Ceres rode down onto the plain before the city with a dozen men. Lord West wasn't among them, but his nephew was, a white pennant tied to his spear. The others were all volunteers, there to ensure that if this went wrong, Ceres might still get back to the army. They stopped halfway to the Empire's army, and at Ceres's signal, Gerant stuck the pennant in the ground.

They waited, and waited. Ceres could feel the tension building amongst the others there. There was no way of knowing how the Empire's army would react. Only the fact that she knew Lucious let her sit there on horseback with confidence. There were only two ways this would go. Either he would come to talk to them, or he would send his army forward to try to capture them, letting hers charge it once it was beyond the trenches. This was the best move they could make.

Finally, a group of soldiers rode forward from the Empire's lines. Lucious was at their head. Ceres forced herself to remain in place rather than charging forward to attack him. There would be time for that later. For now, she had a battle to win, and possibly a war, so she settled for glaring at Lucious as he came closer.

He drew his horse to a halt, looking every inch the noble prince as he sat there in his golden armor. Only the collection of rough-looking thugs he rode with belied it.

"It seems a long way to come just to surrender," Lucious said with a laughing gesture at their flag.

"Maybe I'm offering you a chance to surrender," Ceres countered. "Yield now, and I'll see that you get a fair trial for the things you've done, Lucious."

She saw Lucious sneer. "I'd say I'd missed you, Ceres, but I try not to think about peasants. You should have known when to stay dead. Did you want something, or are we just here to exchange pleasantries?"

Ceres gestured to the horsemen behind her. "You can see I didn't come back alone," she said. "Step aside. Remove your army from the field. There doesn't have to be bloodshed. We both know that you're too much of a coward to want to risk your skin."

"Watch your mouth, girl," Lucious snapped back. "The only skin at risk is yours when we catch you. Maybe I'll have it removed bit by bit and hung up in one of the galleries as a warning."

"You'd have to have it done," Ceres said. "You certainly don't have the fighting skills to ever best me."

"Still challenging your betters?" Lucious retorted. "I could cut you down any time I chose."

Maybe he actually believed it. Certainly, Ceres knew, Lucious would never admit to anything else. In fact, she'd been counting on it.

"Then why don't you prove it?" Ceres said. "Let's settle this one to one. No armies, just single combat. If I win, your army moves out of the way and lets us take Delos."

"And when I cut you down?" Lucious asked.

"Mine turns around and goes home," Ceres said. "You get to be the prince who saved Delos without bloodshed."

Lucious looked as though he was looking for a way out then. He was good at making threats, but he had to know by now that Ceres was the better fighter. She'd bested him before, after all.

"If you refuse," Ceres said, "I'll have men shout the same challenge loud enough that your whole army can hear it. They'll know they're fighting for a coward. What do you think that will do for their morale?"

She saw Lucious flush then, but she still doubted that he would do more than storm off. This wasn't about that. This was about riling him. She wanted to anger him, and taunt him. Anything to get his army to move out of its defensive position to attack hers.

To her surprise, though, Lucious nodded curtly.

"Very well," he said. "Sundown. Single combat. The loser's army to disband. Though I make no promises about what will happen after that. If I can hunt your rabble down, I will."

"You have to beat me first," Ceres said. "I'll see you at sundown."

CHAPTER TWENTY

"It's a lot of people to bring in at once," Anka said, as she walked the corridors of the rebellion's current hideout. She was trying her best to keep her anger in check, and to get Yeralt to see her point of view, but so far, the argument wasn't going well.

"You wanted more people," Yeralt countered, "so I *found* more people."

"You hired them, you mean?" Anka shot back. "You threw Thanos's gold around and let in anyone who showed up?"

Anka guessed that the merchant's son probably wouldn't see the difference. There was no doubting his commitment to overthrowing the Empire, but he often didn't seem to understand how things really were for the poorest of Delos.

"If you want people who know how to fight, you have to pay for them," Yeralt said, as if it were obvious.

Anka saw Sartes ahead in the press of bodies that now filled the underground hideaway. The sight of him calmed her a little. In spite of his age, he seemed to understand the realities of life better than some of the others there. Maybe it was because of the time he'd spent as a conscript. Certainly, his idea to attack the Stade had been a good one. The combatlords were already teaching the others there more about fighting than they could ever have learned otherwise.

"Sartes," Anka said in exasperation. "Explain to Yeralt why it's a bad idea to simply hire in all the fighters we need."

"Where did you get them?" Sartes asked, walking up to the pair.

It was the right question. The sensible question. One that the merchant's son didn't seem to have asked, and that Anka should have.

"My father has people he hires when he wants caravans protected," Yeralt replied, "and I know where to look to find fighting men."

"So they're mercenaries?" Sartes said.

"Or tavern grade thugs," Anka put in.

"Does it matter what they are if they'll fight?" Yeralt said. Anka could hear the annoyance there now. "We give them gold, they fight the Empire. It's easy."

"Until someone comes along with more gold," Anka tried to explain.

She saw the merchant's son shake his head. "You worry too much, Anka. We've grown more in the last few days than in the year before it. Edrin says that the raid on the warehouse went well. Oreth will find us ships. Hannah has been talking to whole networks of informants we didn't know about, now that we have the gold to spend loosening tongues."

"Discreetly, I hope," Anka said.

Yeralt sighed, and Anka knew she'd gone too far. "Of course discreetly. Look, Anka, the others think this is a good idea. We're sick of waiting and being cautious. When a business doesn't expand, it stagnates, or worse, it collapses."

"A lot more's at stake than coin here," Anka said. She tried to be a little more conciliatory, but it was probably too late for that. "I'm not saying we sit and do nothing. I'm saying that we have to do this *right*."

"And we are," Yeralt said. "We know how to do this, and we've decided. Now, I have to get back before I'm missed. I'm going to try to find another route into the city for supplies. There are too many to funnel through my father's caravans."

Anka watched the merchant's son go, trying to contain her frustration. There was a point past which she couldn't afford to be angry. She had to hold things together. Bizarrely, her time in the slaver's pen had helped her with that. It had taught her not to show what she felt. It had taught her that there were worse things than any petty issues that might come. It had shown her what was at stake.

"He doesn't get it," Anka said, when Yeralt was gone. "For all his businesses, he doesn't understand. Please tell me you do, Sartes."

Sartes nodded. "There are too many people to be sure who they all are. Mostly, they'll all be people who want to help the rebellion. Maybe people who always wanted to but weren't sure of the best way to do it."

"But some of them won't be," Anka said, grateful that someone else got the danger. "When the rebellion was still fairly small, I could know who everybody was. If I didn't know, at least one of the people I knew would. Now, people walk past me and I just have to accept that they're with us. That they aren't spies or criminals or worse."

Sartes shrugged. "Part of what makes the rebellion great is that it does accept anybody. We don't turn people away because of their past. This only works if we make it a movement for everyone, until one day the Emperor wakes up and he's the only one not in the rebellion."

Anka smiled at that. "I like that idea, although I'm not going to let Lucious into the rebellion."

"No one's asking you to," Sartes said. "I don't think he's the joining type."

"But plenty of others are," Anka said. "Come with me, would you? I want to see what we're getting for Thanos's gold."

She led the way up through the tunnels, out of an exit that led into a tenement building. There were people waiting there, training with weapons or simply sitting around with nowhere else to go. There was a bench in one corner, where men and women were lining up to receive weapons and gold.

Anka walked across, regarding the man who stood at the front of the line coolly. He had the scars of a man who'd been in a lot of fights, and the slightly ruddy skin of a man who drank too much. There was something about him that set Anka's teeth on edge.

"What's your name?" Anka asked.

"What's it matter to you?" the prospective recruit countered.

"It matters because I'm trying to decide if I want you in my rebellion," Anka said. "I'm Anka. You ask around here, and you'll find out who I am. I want to know who you are so I can ask about *you*."

"I'm Hern, out of the fifteenth regiment. I deserted and came back to the city, joined one of the gangs. That what you want to know about me, girl?"

Anka tried not to match the tone of hostility there. "You say you were in a gang? What were you? A thief? A murderer?"

"What I am is willing to fight the Empire," he replied. "I used to be an enforcer for the Second Streets. Is that good enough for you?"

Anka wanted to say no, but instead, she just gestured him forward to the table. She walked away with Sartes at her side.

"Where do we draw the line, Sartes?" she asked. "We know we wouldn't let the likes of Lucious in, so there are some people we won't tolerate, but who? Criminals? We're all criminals by the Empire's definition. Soldiers? You're a former soldier, and so are all the conscripts who joined us. Yeralt's right, we need all the people we can get, but mercenaries and thugs? We can't trust them."

"So don't trust them," Sartes said, and he made it sound so obvious. "You can't question everyone who wants to join personally, but you can ask someone to vouch for them before they join. You can make sure that only the people who need to know things are told them."

"You're too young to have so little trust in people," Anka said.

Sartes shrugged. "There are plenty of people I trust. I trust you."

"It seems as though a lot of people are trusting me these days," Anka said. "I have to make the right decisions, or it could mean people's lives."

"You've been making the right calls so far," Sartes said. "You organized the ambush in the burial ground and the freeing of the combatlords. We have the army's weapons and Thanos's gold."

"You played a pretty big role in those too," Anka said. "How's the weapon sorting going?"

Sartes shook his head. "My father says that the Empire needs to employ better smiths. He also said I might be able to help you more here."

Anka smiled. "He's probably right. It looks as though I could use all the help I can get."

She stood there, and Sartes could hear something left unsaid in the silence.

"What is it?" Sartes asked. "I mean, if you can tell me."

"I'll always be able to tell you things," Anka said. "If there's one person in the rebellion I *don't* have to worry about being a spy, it's you. It's not that."

"Then what?" Sartes asked.

"Sartes, I have news." Anka stood there, uncertain for a moment, standing next to a window and looking out on the city. Should she say this now? "You were talking about things people need to know. Well, I don't know if I should tell you this, because it's just a rumor, and I didn't even believe it when I heard it."

"What is it?" Sartes asked. "Is it about the army?"

"In a way," Anka said. There were enough rumors about the army outside the city that Sartes must have heard some of them. "I've spent the morning listening to what's happening out there, piecing things together. The army formed up in front of the city yesterday, because it had heard that there was a force coming under Lord West."

"So there's going to be a battle?" Sartes asked.

Anka spread her hands, trying to think of the best way to say this. "We thought so, but there's been an offer of single combat to settle it. Lucious has sent a champion, and on the other side… I can hardly believe I'm saying it."

"What is it?" Sartes asked.

"It's Ceres," Anka said, and she could see the shock on Sartes's face even as she said it. "Ceres is the one fighting on the other side."

She took his shoulders in her hands.

"She is alive, Sartes."

CHAPTER TWENTY ONE

With sundown looming, Ceres prepared herself. She sharpened her sword, made sure the dagger Eoin had given her was still strong, went through the motions of the islanders' way of fighting, stretched her muscles, and waited.

No one disturbed her.

They all seemed to know instinctively to leave her in peace for it.

Finally, sunset came.

Down below, Ceres could see men coming out from the Empire's army, moving out to the center of the plain. For a moment, she thought that perhaps Lucious might be trying a surprise attack—but they came out with spades and rushes, digging a series of pits that they filled and then set light to, illuminating a section of the field even as the sun faded.

They were making a ring to fight in.

"It's time," Ceres said, mounting her horse. "Lord West, if this goes wrong—"

"It won't," he replied. "Remember who you are. *What* you are."

Ceres nodded. Heart pounding, feeling the eyes of thousands of men upon her, she mounted her horse, kicked, and rode.

Around her, her army formed, lifting banners high in a kind of salute, cheering as she rode through the pathway they created. She felt as if she were back in the Stade, with the crowd roaring in appreciation as she stepped onto the sands.

She rode down in the direction of that impromptu arena, and some of her men followed her. Not many. Not enough that it would look like an attack, but enough to form a crowd. Enough to prevent an attack on her by Lucious's forces.

Ceres dismounted by the edge, hobbling her horse. She stepped between two of the fires, into the brightly lit space beyond. Then she waited.

She saw Lucious ride forward at the heart of a cluster of men to match her own. Another horse beside him carried a servant or weapon carrier wrapped up in a thick cloak.

When they reached the ring, though, it was the servant who dismounted, not Lucious.

Ceres felt a hint of outrage rise in her chest.

This was replaced with dread as she saw the size of the servant, who stood far taller than she did, far taller than Lucious.

"What's this?" Ceres demanded.

She heard Lucious laugh.

"I'm a prince, you stupid peasant. You think I fight my own battles? I have champions for that! Don't worry, though, I've brought you an old friend."

His "servant" threw aside the cloak then. Ceres saw dark, muscled skin, criss-crossed by scars and tattoos and only partly covered by armor. The man there held a staff with crescent blades at either end, but it was his dead, baleful gaze that held her attention most.

Ceres heard the intake of breath from the crowd around her. They knew who this was, just as she did. The only man to ever best her in the Stade. The one who'd been about to kill her when they'd dragged her away to the prison ship.

The Last Breath.

The combatlord known as the Last Breath stepped into the circle of flames, and while the fire reflected from his dual-bladed weapon, Ceres heard Lucious laugh.

Ceres felt a thrill of fear as the Last Breath stood there before her. She found herself remembering the sight of him standing over her, his weapon poised for the final blow that had never come in the Stade.

It was obvious that her opponent remembered it too.

"I kill my enemies," he said, sending his bladed staff into a contemptuous spin. "All of them, except you. This time, I make that right."

Ceres pushed back the residue of fear, remembering the things that had happened to her since. She'd learned all the islanders had to offer, but more than that, she'd learned who she was.

"You won't find it that easy," she promised him. "I've learned a lot since then."

She heard him laugh, and the sound was like a boom of thunder in the dusk. Midway through it, the Last Breath attacked, and the crowd roared.

Ceres was ready for it this time in a way she hadn't been in the Stade. There, her powers had deserted her. Now, energy flooded through her, lending her the speed to flow out of the way of a kick that would have sent her back into the fiery ring.

She parried and dodged, moving aside from the Last Breath's strikes. He was still frighteningly fast for such a big man, but this time she was as fast as he was, and she wasn't going to be overwhelmed the way she had been in the Stade.

She could see the patterns now, understand the furious malice behind it, seeing it like sharp spikes at the edges of her awareness. She sank into the feeling of the fight, letting herself go the way Eoin and the others had taught her.

She leaned back from a sweep of the crescent blades, dropped further to avoid a swinging kick, and then rolled smoothly back to her feet. She struck out with her long blade, forcing the Last Breath to parry, then stepped back to avoid the counter.

She kept moving, feeling the heat of the fires at her back as she went. The Last Breath rushed her, obviously trying to force her back into that heat, and Ceres dodged, bringing her blades together to block a stroke that tried to catch her as she angled away.

She cut out, drawing a line of blood on the Last Breath's arm.

He stared at it in fury, and Ceres knew he would be thinking back to what had happened after she'd cut him in their fight in the Stade.

Sure enough, he came at her then, swinging his staff in blow after blow.

Part of his skill, Ceres realized now, was in not having an obvious rhythm to his attacks. Most fighters struck and moved in clear beats, and anyone else using a weapon like the one the Last Breath did would have swung it back and forth, back and forth. He seemed to instinctively realized the danger of that, the blades never quite there when they should have been.

For a moment, Ceres felt herself falling out of the place where the power flowed into her. It was as though the world around her sped up, and suddenly the Last Breath was everywhere. Ceres parried one blow, felt another graze through the flesh of her side, and then found herself caught across the back of the legs by the haft of her opponent's weapon.

Ceres lay on her back for a moment or two, looking up as the Last Breath stood there, his weapon raised high. The firelight glinted from the steel, the flames seeming to reflect in his eyes. It was too close, far too close, to the way things had been in the Stade.

Only this time, there wouldn't be any reprieve. There was no one to heed the calls of the crowd, or to decide that it would be better if she died quietly, away from other eyes. Stephania wasn't there this time, but Lucious was, looking on with obvious glee from the sidelines.

"Ceres! Ceres! Ceres!" she heard the men on her side chanting, as if trying to revive her just with the calls.

"This time," the Last Breath said, "you die."

110

Except this wasn't the Stade. Ceres understood the power that lay within her now. It wasn't some strange, unknown thing that came and went as it wished. It was a part of her. It was a part of who she was.

So when she called it up within her again, it was there waiting.

She rolled smoothly, moving out of the way of the Last Breath's blow and kicking out to force him back.

Ceres leapt back onto her feet and then went on the attack. She thrust with her dagger and cut with her sword, never staying in one spot, never giving the Last Breath a chance to settle. She spun inside the arc of his weapon, opening another wound on her opponent then moving out again.

She saw a moment of balance and seized the opening. Ceres kicked out at the haft of the Last Breath's weapon, lifting her leg high and catching it in the middle. Before, such an attack might not have done anything, but now Ceres heard the crack as the pole arm gave way beneath her strike. She saw the Last Breath stare at it as though Ceres had just killed the only thing he had cared about in the world.

He roared, clutching one half of the broken weapon and swinging it in a figure eight like an axe. He swung at Ceres's head and she ducked, cutting with her dagger as she moved past him. The Last Breath swung again and Ceres leaned back, slicing another cut into his arm.

The Last Breath didn't have an obvious rhythm to his attacks, but there *was* a rhythm to it, hidden under the fury and the cunning. It was hummingbird fast, varying and shifting, but it was there.

Ceres would never have been able to pick it out if she hadn't spent so long with the forest folk trying their different skills on her. She would never have been fast enough to keep up with it if she hadn't learned to accept what she was.

As it was, she fit in with it as smoothly as a dance.

She spun and ducked and leapt, always a beat ahead of the Last Breath's furious swings. With each movement, she struck out, wounding him again and again, wearing him down the way a hunter might wear down some great beast. It wasn't cruelty; it was simply that, even now, Ceres knew that trying to finish things would only open her up to a lightning fast riposte.

The Last Breath feigned a stumbling step, but Ceres saw it for what it was. She took a half step forward, then pushed back, dodging as the combatlord threw himself forward in a desperate strike. Ceres struck with both her swords, catching the Last Breath across his back.

111

She saw him stumble, his weapon falling from his hand. Even so, he stood, somehow defying the wounds that would have killed another man.

"Yield," Ceres said. "Let this end. Don't let Lucious keep using you."

The Last Breath shook his head and leapt at her.

Ceres reached out, and her power flowed from her into the Last Breath.

She watched the shock in his eyes as stone flourished in place of his skin, freezing him in place. The stone was as thick and dark as his skin, basalt and obsidian, matching every scar and nick on him.

Ceres could have left him like that, but some part of her didn't trust the combatlord even as a block of dark granite. She kicked out and set the statue rocking back and forth on the hard earth.

It toppled almost slowly, and when it hit the ground, Ceres heard the crack as it shattered, breaking into a dozen or more pieces.

Ceres stood, making sure that both armies could see her there as she called out.

"You've lost, Lucious! Surrender the city, or be branded the oath breaker you are!"

Something flew at Ceres from out of the dark. She dodged on instinct, and an arrow whispered past her cheek before thudding into the dirt. Ceres ran forward, leaping over the nearest fire, setting off in pursuit of Lucious.

He was already riding away, pushing his horse to greater speed than Ceres could hope to match. She could hear him shouting out what sounded like orders as he rode, although she couldn't make out the words from there.

Behind her, she saw her army advancing. Lord West had obviously seen Lucious's betrayal, and wasn't about to risk leaving Ceres to face the Empire's whole army. The horsemen of the North Coast charged in a long line, apparently not caring about the danger of the Empire's trenches if it meant keeping Ceres safe.

Yet the Empire's army didn't move to attack. Nor did it stand ready to receive the charge. Instead, while Ceres watched, its phalanxes wheeled and started to march back through the open gates of the city.

"Quick!" Ceres called to the approaching riders. "We have to catch them before they get inside."

They could win it here. Even if Lucious wouldn't keep his word, if they could hit their army from behind while it was on the move, they had a chance to break its ranks. Her riders thundered down toward Ceres, and they didn't slow. Instead, she saw Gerant leading a spare horse, and Ceres understood.

She caught the reins as it rode past her, leaping up and hauling herself into the saddle. She kicked her horse on, trying to make it to the Empire's ranks before they could enter the city. There was no way they could all make it inside now, and some of them seemed to have gathered by the trenches.

Except they didn't form defensive ranks. Instead, Ceres saw the flicker of flaming torches. They threw them into the trenches, and fire roared up.

There must have been oil in the pits. That was the only explanation for the great walls of flame that surged up in front of her charging army. Even as far away as she was, Ceres could feel the heat of it.

So could the horses, it seemed. Ceres saw them shy away, the charge faltering. Many reared up, and it was only the riding skills of her men that kept them from falling from the saddle. Around her, Ceres heard men trying to calm their horses, and horses snorting in fear at the flames ahead. She had to lean down, gripping her own reins tightly as she pulled her horse to a halt.

There was no way past the flames. Even where there had seemed to be thin bridges of land between the trenches before, there were no gaps now. Oil had obviously been spread over the ground too. All Ceres could do was sit there in the saddle, watching the fires burn.

There was the whir of arrows in the night, and somewhere beside her, Ceres saw a man fall. Other arrows thudded into shields. One caught a horse, and the beast went down, taking its rider with it.

"Pull back," she called. "We're in bow shot here. Pull *back*!"

Her army retreated, away from the trenches, back up the hillside they'd come from. All Ceres could do up there was watch as the fires burned down to embers, their orange glow spreading over the ground before the city.

They illuminated its gates perfectly. Those were massive, stone built, and very firmly shut now behind Lucious's army. Above them, Ceres thought she could see a flash of gold illuminated in the firelight: Lucious looking out, probably feeling very pleased by it all.

Ceres turned to Lord West, and she could see he was thinking the same thing as she.

"Make camp and set watches on all of the city's gates," she said. "We're going to have to take Delos by siege."

CHAPTER TWENTY TWO

Lucious waited in front of the throne like a condemned man while his father bellowed.

"A *siege*?" the king demanded. "How could you let it come to a siege?"

Right then, standing before the court with most of the nobles of Delos watching, Lucious had never felt so angry with them all. He was still wearing his golden armor, still carrying the sword he'd worn on the battlefield, and a part of him wanted to rush among them then, cutting them down just for daring to be there while his father tried to humiliate him in front of them.

But he didn't do it. Instead, he stood there, his armor spattered with mud, looking far from his glorious best in the throne room while his father the king shouted. The nobles around him were silent, as though sensing that any sound might bring royal wrath down on them.

"You were supposed to go out and give battle to them, you stupid boy!"

"We might have lost if we'd done that," Lucious countered. "There were more of them than we anticipated, and Ceres—" He didn't finish that, even though he could see the nobles leaning in, looking for news of the girl. He still wasn't sure *what* had happened with Ceres. What he'd seen her do there in the ring of flames made no sense.

"You might have crushed them as you were supposed to!" King Claudius said, bringing his hand down hard on the arm of his throne. The one beside it was empty; Lucious couldn't look to his mother for help tonight. Indeed, many of the ladies of the court were absent, as if this were beneath them to see. "When you had the fire pits dug, I thought it was a sign that you were maturing as a leader, but they were meant to cut off your foes' escape, not give you time to run!"

"I ran because there was no other option!" Lucious insisted, raising his voice to match his father's. How *dare* he treat Lucious like this in front of all the others? "After they saw the Last Breath lose, the men wouldn't have stood and fought."

Lucious could practically feel the tension in the nobles around them. Men shifted in place, as though wishing they could be anywhere else. Cowards.

"You mean that you wouldn't," the king said. "As for this business of single combat, you should have thought about the implications of it before you accepted the challenge from that girl."

"She was supposed to *lose*," Lucious snapped back. There was just the faintest intake of breath from those around them.

"Watch your tone, boy," his father said. "Remember who is king here."

Lucious remembered, just as he reminded himself that sooner or later, his father would die, and he would be king in his turn. Then there would be no one to talk to him like this.

"Ceres had already lost to the Last Breath once," Lucious said. "He should have beaten her easily, and then probably that fool Lord West would have disbanded, because he believes in honor so much. At the very least, we would have been able to parade what was left of her through the streets to break the rebellion's spirit."

"All of which sounds like a fine plan," his father said. "Except for the part where she cut your man to pieces."

"She used some trickery, or magic, or something to do it," Lucious insisted. "How was I to know that she could do something like that?"

"A good commander learns the facts of the situation before he acts," the king said. "Didn't I provide you with enough warning? Didn't I tell you what you needed to do? You were to go out and meet them. If you'd judged it right, you could have ambushed them as they made their way to the city; cut them down before they even got close. Instead, you stood and waited beneath the safety of the walls."

Fury rose in Lucious then, sweet and hot, but explosive too. The words poured out before he could stop them. "Maybe you should have gotten someone else to command the army then! Oh, no, wait, you couldn't, could you? You were too busy sitting here, your generals are missing, and as for Thanos—"

"Enough!" King Claudius roared. "I have defended you at every turn, Lucious. I gave you this command because I thought you might be the one to put down this rebellion the way it deserves to be put down. But it seems you weren't capable of dealing with it, and now *I* must be the one to deal with our city being under siege."

"Not Thanos?" Lucious said with a smirk. "It's almost as if you don't trust him when it comes to Ceres, or something, Father."

"Thanos is as loyal as any man," the king declared. "And at least he knows how to command properly. He survived Haylon, and the Stade. Give me one good reason, Lucious, why I shouldn't send

116

you from this room in disgrace and give him your command under me."

Lucious almost didn't say anything, but his anger had gone from something burning red to something cool and white and dangerous. He'd spent a lot of gold learning everything he knew, and to miss an opportunity this good would be far too foolish.

"I think you might want to reserve judgment, my king," Lucious said. "At least until you've heard what I have to tell you."

"And why would I do that?" his father said.

"Because then, you might change your mind about who you want in charge of your armies, and who you trust."

***

Thanos sat, looking at his wife, feeling amazed that his life could have taken the turns it had. She'd said she had things to tell him tonight, and he was trying to guess at what they might be. He knew Stephania liked to collect secrets.

He was still wondering about it, dining quietly with Stephania, when the servants hammered on the door to his rooms.

"Prince Thanos, come at once. The king requires your presence on an urgent matter."

"Ignore them," Stephania said, reaching out to close her hand over his arm as if to hold him there. "There are things I need to talk to you about, and tell you."

Thanos heard more thudding fists on the door. "Prince Thanos, the king said that there can be no delay."

Thanos made a face and leaned over to kiss his wife. "I don't think we're getting a choice in this. It's probably to do with whatever's got the army in front of the city. And you keep saying that I can't afford to anger the king."

"No," Stephania agreed. "Try to remember that." She looked down at her relatively simple day dress. "Give me a chance to dress properly, and I'll come with you."

Thanos waved that away. "You shouldn't have your evening ruined for this." He took her hand and kissed it. "I'll be back soon, then you can tell me whatever your news is. I bet it will be better than the king's."

"It will," Stephania promised.

Thanos rose and headed for the door. He wasn't really dressed for an audience with the king, in just a relatively simple tunic and breeches, but it sounded too urgent for anything more formal.

The men outside weren't servants, but members of the royal bodyguard.

"What's this?" Thanos said.

"It's a vital matter," one of the men said. "We need to hurry."

So Thanos hurried, half expecting to be led in the direction of the king's private chambers. Instead, though, he saw that they were heading in the direction of the throne room, hurrying along at something just short of a run.

"Is it something to do with the army?" Thanos asked, hoping to understand what was going on. He figured that fighting men might at least give him a clue.

"Forgive us, Prince Thanos," the bodyguard said, "but the king said he would explain once you got there."

Thanos wasn't sure what to make of that, but he knew there was no point in testing the loyalty of the royal bodyguard. Besides, thanks to the speed they were walking at, they would be at the throne room soon enough.

They reached it, and the guards at the doors let them inside. Thanos could feel straightaway that something was wrong. There was a hush there that there shouldn't have been, even if the king had demanded quiet. The nobles there looked shocked, even angry, as they stood to either side of the hall. He heard the sound of the doors slamming shut behind him like a tombstone falling over.

Something had gone wrong.

"What is it?" Thanos demanded. "What's happened?"

Then he saw Lucious's face; saw the look of triumph there, and he understood. By that point though, the royal bodyguards had already formed up around him with their swords drawn. There would be no chance to run, and unarmed, even Thanos couldn't fight so many.

King Claudius sat perfectly still, and to Thanos, he seemed caught halfway between anger and sadness. "What happened? What happened is that you betrayed us."

"And who says that?" Thanos countered. It was his only chance now. "Lucious? You know he'd say anything to cause trouble. He's probably just looking for revenge for beating him senseless, still."

"That's what I suspected," the king replied. He gestured to one side of the court. "Until Lucious brought me this man."

A ragged-looking man stepped forward from the crowd, wearing a soldier's uniform. It was too new to be original, and Thanos guessed Lucious had given it to him for effect.

"Say again what you told us," the king said. "*Say* it."

"Prince Thanos joined the rebels on Haylon," the man said. "He helped them to burn our ships and attack our men. Do I... when do I get my reward?"

"You hear that?" Thanos said. "He's only saying it because Lucious paid him."

"That is possible," the king said, "but when he came forward, others brought forward their suspicions. A guard mentioned that you had requisitioned gold from the treasury for the army, but there is no record of it reaching them. A bird from Haylon has arrived informing me of General *Haven's* progress there, when I'm sure I sent Olliant. At the same time, a junior member of my chamberlain's staff tells me that you were in his office the morning that fleet sailed, and Lucious says he saw you out there. Of course, I will have this wretch tortured to ensure he is telling the truth, but we both know what he will say, *don't we?* After all, you have already tried to murder my son!"

The king stood then, and with the added effect of the dais, he loomed over Thanos.

"You are a traitor, Thanos. Admit it. Or maybe I'll make you watch the torture. You're soft enough that I'm sure you wouldn't want that."

"I'm soft?" Thanos said. "Maybe it's just you who's forgotten what it's like to have any humanity. You ordered General Draco to slaughter men, women, and children on Haylon. You've had Lucious butchering your own people in the name of putting down the rebellion. It's evil, and it needs to be stopped!"

"So you've been helping to stop it?" the king demanded.

Thanos stood proudly, because there was no point in trying to deny it anymore. "Yes. Yes, I have. And you might kill me for it, but there will be a dozen more to take my place. A hundred. The more brutal you try to be, the more the rebellion will rise up, until you and everyone like you are swept away!"

Thanos saw the king, his father, bring his hands together, looking down as though searching for some kind of answer. Then he shook his head.

"A fine speech, but an empire like this exists only because there is order within it. Only because it is strong. I tried to explain that to you once before, and you failed to learn the lesson. I gave you a chance, and you have thrown that chance back in my face! Even now, I suspect that you would cut me down if I gave you the opportunity."

Thanos looked him squarely in the eye. "If it is the only way to stop you."

"Then you are the one who must be stopped," King Claudius said. "Take Thanos to a cell. Tomorrow, he will be taken by boat to the Isle of Prisoners. Once he is there, I will decide a suitable way for him to die."

Thanos tried to struggle, because he couldn't *not* struggle. He swung a punch at one royal bodyguard, then tried to grab a weapon from another. There were too many, though, and they piled in together, dragging him to the ground. Even some of the nobles joined in, as though wanting to show their loyalty. They punched and kicked at him: people he'd known, former friends.

Then Lucious was there, holding a weighted club. "I've wanted to watch you fall for a long time. Now I get to."

He swung it, and darkness exploded through Thanos's skull.

CHAPTER TWENTY THREE

The nobles of the North Coast had looked at Ceres with respect before, but now it felt more like awe as she sat amid the campfires and the hastily erected tents. Half of them didn't seem to dare to speak to her after what she'd done to the Last Breath, while the other half treated her as if she were something far more than human.

Then again, she supposed she was. It was just that it took some getting used to.

Right now, she was sitting around a fire with Lord West and a few of his men. The fire wasn't anywhere near as intense as the flame-filled trenches had been, but even so, it was a reminder of them. The lord of the North Coast had fetched Ceres a platter of trail bread, venison, and beans himself, and had tasted it before he'd handed it to her.

"You don't have to do that," Ceres tried to tell him, but the older man shook his head.

"I do," he insisted. "My family swore to lay down their lives if necessary for your ancestors, and there are more than enough poisoners around Delos for it to be a risk. We cannot afford to lose you."

"These are your men," Ceres said. "They fight for you."

That just got another shake of Lord West's head. "They fight because you are here, my lady. Because you have shown them that there are powers out there greater than the strength of the Empire."

"It's not as though I could take on the Empire alone though," Ceres said. It might have been nice if she could have turned all of their opponents to stone, taken all the risks for herself rather than pulling others into it, but her powers didn't work like that. They took effort. "We've only come this far because you're all here."

"I just hope the rebellion is waiting for us," Lord West said. "We cannot afford a long siege."

"Lucious won't dare bring his men out to face us now," Ceres said. "Trust me, he's a coward at heart. He's nice and safe behind a wall, and he'll stay there until someone pries him out."

"With respect, my lady," Lord West said. "That's all he needs to do. We are horsemen. On open ground, we can run down the strongest foes, but horses cannot climb walls. And they need to eat, just as their riders do."

Ceres understood then. "Lucious has been ravaging the countryside for a long time now. There won't be any food to find.

I'm sorry, Lord West. I've fought in the Stade, but I'm not used to how armies work."

Lord West gestured to the others there. "You've got us this far, and you *did* best Lucious's man. If he'd taken the challenge himself, we might not have this problem now. But if you wouldn't mind my saying, my lady?"

"You don't have to ask, Lord West," Ceres said, taking a bite out of her food. After all that had happened today, she was ravenous. "I don't want to be someone like King Claudius. Someone people are afraid to say things to in case they don't like them."

"That's good," Lord West said. "Then you have to understand that there are more problems than just the food, although that is significant. Delos *can* outwait us. And when it comes to winter, it will be hard. But it might not last that long. My hope was that the rebellion would rise up when we reached the city, and we would have it in our possession before any of the other legions of the Empire's army could come to reinforce it."

"But now, with us stuck outside the city, we're easy prey," Ceres said. "Caught between the hammer and the anvil."

"Exactly," Lord West said. "My men have shot down what messenger birds they could, but we cannot be certain they got them all, and we do not control the docks."

"They could simply send a messenger that way, or even bring reinforcements back by boat," Ceres said. She understood the magnitude of the situation now. They needed to take the city quickly. "All the gates will be well guarded, so we can't just slip into the city, but—"

"What is it?" Lord West asked.

"There might be a way," Ceres said. "The rebellion has always had secret ways into the city, and I know some of the old ones, from when Rexus was alive."

"We wouldn't be able to sneak the army that close to the walls," Lord West said. "With this many men and horses, someone would spot the movement, and doing it by night is dangerous anyway, simply with the numbers of the men."

Ceres stood. "I'm not talking about sneaking the whole army in," she said. "Just me."

"You?" Lord West shook his head. "What if something were to happen? No, we need you."

"To sit out here with you until the rest of the Empire's army arrives?" Ceres said. "No. I got you into this. I should be the one to get you into the city, too."

"You're too valuable," Lord West said.

"We've already established that I don't really know how to command an army," Ceres said. "But I *do* know the ways into the city, and there will be people in the rebellion who trust me." She thought of her brother, and her father. Of Anka. "Hopefully, people I've wanted to see for a long time now. They'll listen to me, but if you or one of your men goes, what will they see? A noble trying to give them orders? I'm the best person for this job, while *you're* the best person to ensure that when I get one of the city's gates open at dawn, your men are ready to respond."

"I still don't like this," Lord West said. "I should send men with you."

"You know that would only increase the risk," Ceres said. "The best thing you can do right now is trust me. It's not as though you can stop me, unless you're going to have me guarded day and night."

Lord West hesitated for several seconds and then stood, clasping her hand. "Very well. But if you're not back by noon, my lady, I will assault the walls to get you back."

"You've already told me that horses can't climb," Ceres pointed out.

"They can't," Lord West said. "So you'd better make sure that you succeed."

***

Ceres crept toward the city's walls with only the faintest points of light to guide her. There were the dying embers in the fire pits outside the walls, the pinpricks of starlight above, and the glow of torches belonging to the sentries the Empire had set on Delos's walls. Ceres was grateful for the last of those, because at least it told her where the watchers were likely to be.

She was grateful that it was a moonless night, too. It meant that, wrapped in a cloak, she barely left a trace as she crept across the open ground between her camp and the city. She hoped that any watcher would just see one more shadow against the grass, and not catch any glimmer from the armor that lay beneath.

She'd padded that so it wouldn't make a sound as she moved. The last thing Ceres wanted was to be all but invisible, but to make so much noise that the Empire's sentries could find her anyway. She picked her steps as carefully as she could too, feeling for twigs or broken ground that might give her away.

"I just hope there's someone there when I get there," Ceres murmured to herself.

When Rexus had led the rebellion, there had been set points where its members would look out for people who wanted to enter the city secretly, and set signs to let them know that a friend was approaching. Ceres had known all of them, because Rexus had made sure that she knew.

Now, though, Ceres had no way of knowing if the spots were still the same. The signals might have changed, or worse, the Empire might have found some of the routes and started watching them, capturing any rebels foolish enough to still use them. When Rexus had been in charge, they'd had to change several of the routes for exactly that reason. Ceres had no way of knowing which ones were still current.

She kept on toward the walls. Perhaps someone else could have done this, in spite of what she'd said to Lord West, but the truth was that she was the one with the best chance to persuade the rebellion.

Ceres skirted around the edge of one of the fire pits, and heard a noise somewhere above. On instinct, she threw herself flat.

"What's that?" someone said from a spot on the wall that had seemed dark and empty a moment before.

"Probably nothing," another voice said. "You've been jumping at shadows all night."

Ceres saw a guard then, lighting a previously cold torch. She could imagine him looking out over the grass beyond the walls, and tried to stay as still as possible, hoping that the darkness of her cloak would hide her.

"You see? There's nothing there. Now, we need to get back to our patrols. The captain will kill us if he catches us playing dice."

Ceres dared to move again as she saw the light move off, but she didn't move quickly. Instead, she crawled her way toward the base of the wall, not caring how long it took. She couldn't afford any more risks.

It seemed to take forever before her fingers touched stone and mortar, and even longer before Ceres found the spot she wanted. Above, there was a section where a gate for goods might once have been that now looked walled up. The bricks could still be moved from inside though, and when she'd left, the rebellion had sent people to watch it at night.

Ceres whistled, following a pattern of long and short notes she hoped she'd remembered correctly. The noise seemed far too loud against the silence of the night air. Ceres waited, pressed flat against the wall, hoping that none of the guards had heard.

She kept on waiting, counting her heartbeats, trying to get some sense of the time that was passing. At least a minute went by with no sound from above, and now, along the wall in the distance, Ceres could see the steady light of a torch moving in her direction. She didn't think it was because someone had heard. It wasn't moving fast enough for that, but the light would still be enough to see her by.

She had to make a choice. She could run back into the night, but that movement risked being seen, and she might not get another shot at this. Or she could whistle again. She did, and halfway through she realized that she'd been whistling the wrong sequence. Quickly, she changed it.

The light was moving toward Ceres quicker now. Obviously the guard had heard, but Ceres could hear something too: the scrape of stones moving, followed by the quiet slap of rope falling against stone. A rope ladder came down beside her, and Ceres didn't hesitate.

She clambered up, forcing herself to concentrate on the climb rather than on the light that signaled a rapidly approaching guard. She hurried up the ladder, hauling herself into a small, dimly lit space that was little more than a gap left over by new building and forgotten about. She watched as a man in a rough tunic pulled the stone façade back into place.

He turned to her and drew a knife.

"Who are you, and why are you using out-of-date signal codes? If one of the others had been watching, they probably wouldn't even have recognized them."

Ceres stepped into what little light there was, watching the shock spread across the features of the watcher as she did so.

"My name is Ceres," she said. "And I have returned to lead you."

CHAPTER TWENTY FOUR

Stephania was spending the coin of favors as fast as she dared. Faster, because what she was doing right now might very easily get her killed. When she'd heard what had happened to Thanos, she'd sent her handmaidens out to look for details at once. She'd dressed as carefully as she could, and she'd set out to free him as surely as a warrior in full armor might have set off after some fair maiden in a story.

Except that this wasn't a story, and her husband, the man she loved, was in danger.

Stephania had always told herself that love was a trap; that the only love worth having was for oneself. Now, she was doing things that might get her killed, and all for a man who was trying to bring down the very Empire that had given her such a good life.

It was a kind of madness, but a madness that made so much more sense now. Finally, she was starting to understand what true love meant, and it wasn't what she had thought. It wasn't about possessing another. It wasn't about hurting them when they refused you. It was this… this willingness to give anything for them.

"Even my life," Stephania whispered.

"What's that, my lady?" one of her handmaids asked.

"Nothing," Stephania said. "Milla, I need you to go and find Captain Delvar. Take him this note. If he argues, remind him who saved his head when the father of his last lover wanted to take it. If *that* doesn't work, remind him that I know he hasn't paid the king his cut of the slaving operations he conducted among the Isles of Teeth."

"Yes, my lady."

So many secrets, so many strings of knowledge and obligation that she'd hoarded like a miser. Now, Stephania was running through them almost too fast to keep track of. There had been the secrets spent to find out exactly what had happened in the throne room. There had been the attempts to find out how Lucious had found this soldier, when Stephania thought that she'd disposed of the only link to him. She'd used a noble lady's former indiscretions to find out which part of the dungeons Thanos had been sent to, and a guard captain's dangerous habits to secure access to the upper layers of them.

Now she was walking through them, past cells holding rebels and dissidents, thieves and murderers. They were mostly thrown in together, and Stephania could see men and women huddled in barred spaces seemingly at random. She could practically smell the despair there, mixed in with the sweat and human waste of the place. Would she end there, if this went wrong, or would they simply kill her out of hand?

"This way, my lady," one of the jailors said. His price had been the location for a daughter long believed lost. It was a surprisingly maudlin thing, Stephania thought, for such a rough-looking man. "Ignore all them. They're just not looking forward to what's coming to them."

That was probably death or torture, mutilation or shipment to the Isle of Prisoners. Stephania didn't particularly care which. They didn't matter. Only Thanos mattered to her right then. She would see every one of her servants and friends impaled or tied to an execution pyre before she lost him.

She would even risk it for herself.

Stephania swallowed as she walked down through the dungeons, tasting the scent of the guttering torches that lit it as much as smelling them. She could hear screams, only partly muffled by thick doors, and she guessed that was deliberate, designed to put fear into the prisoners yet to suffer.

"Oh, don't worry," the jailor said, and he seemed to be enjoying Stephania's discomfort far too much. "We won't be working on your husband. Not when there's the Isle of Prisoners waiting for him."

If the circumstances had been different, Stephania would have seen that the man suffered for that comment. As it was, she merely nodded and kept walking. Their route headed down, always down, until it seemed that they must be deep underneath Delos, in a space that sunlight never touched.

"This is as far as I go," the jailor said, pointing. "His cell's that way."

"That wasn't our agreement," Stephania snapped back.

"Well, I want to live to see my daughter, and those royal bodyguards—"

"*What* royal bodyguards?" Stephania asked.

"You didn't think they'd leave him unguarded, did you?" the jailor countered, already walking away.

Stephania stood there and fumed. She hadn't prepared for this. She hadn't planned for this, and she should have. An idiot could have guessed that there might be extra guards at a time like this, but Stephania had been too busy thinking about Thanos. Love could make a fool out of anyone.

She pulled her favorite necklace from around her neck. It was a thing of heavy white gold, dripping with emeralds and sapphires. At least she could plan now. She took a small vial from her dress, carefully avoiding contact with the stones as she dripped the contents on them.

She kept walking and found a door at the end of the corridor, attended by a royal bodyguard seated on a chair, his gilt-edged armor reflecting light from a torch and a naked blade sitting across his knee. Stephania saw him rise as she approached.

"Forgive me, my lady, but the king said that Prince Thanos was to be kept secluded."

"I merely wish to see my husband," Stephania said.

"The king's orders were very clear."

"My *husband* has been accused of being a traitor and dragged away to a cell without my even getting to say goodbye. I would give anything… *anything,* just to be able to speak to him for a moment or two."

"Anything?" the guard asked, and Stephania knew she had him. The royal bodyguards were supposedly incorruptible, but in her experience, no one was. No one except Thanos, perhaps.

Stephania held up the necklace. It was worth more than a man like this would see in his lifetime. Stephania dangled it in her hand.

"Would this be enough?" Stephania asked. "Not even to do anything much. Just to walk away for a few minutes while I speak to the man I love. You can understand love, I'm sure."

"I prefer the kind I can buy," the guard said. His fist closed around the necklace. "But this buys a lot."

He walked away, tossing a key to Stephania as he went. She hurriedly fit it into the lock. Thanos was in there, looking bruised as he sat in a bare stone cell. Stephania ran to him, putting a hand to his cheek.

"Thanos," she said. "How could you be so foolish as to get caught?"

He smiled up at her. "I thought you'd be angry with me for helping the rebels. I thought you'd hate me."

"I could never hate you," Stephania said. "I love you."

After all the lies she'd told in her life, that one truth felt oh so sweet. She kissed him then, long and deep.

"It isn't safe for you to say that right now," Thanos said. "It isn't safe for you to be here, Stephania."

"I don't care," Stephania said.

"You should," Thanos replied. "You should get as far away from my cell as you can and pretend that you hate me, even if you don't. You should be the first to condemn me whenever they speak about me. That way, they won't think you're a traitor along with me."

Stephania smiled at that. Almost no one else who had ever been in her life would have put her first like that. They wouldn't have decided, in a moment when their own life was at stake, that Stephania's life was worth more. It just showed how special Thanos was.

"It's probably a little late for that," Stephania said, pulling Thanos to his feet. "For one thing, I'm carrying your child."

Thanos stopped, stepping back and staring at her in obvious disbelief. "You're pregnant?"

Stephania bit her lip as she nodded. "I'm pregnant."

The world seemed to light up with Thanos's smile. "That's incredible. It's wonderful news!"

Stephania found herself folded into a hug, and she wished that she could stay there like that with Thanos forever. She felt safe like that with him. Wanted. Loved. She could feel tears beginning to roll down her cheeks, because she'd never had anything like this in her life before. She was surprised when she stepped back and found similar tear tracks on Thanos's cheeks.

"We're really going to be parents?" Thanos asked, taking her hands.

Stephania could feel the strength in his touch, but also the gentleness there. "We really are, and I don't care if you have been helping the rebels. None of that matters."

"It matters if they take me away and kill me for it," Thanos said. "Or worse, if they kill you just for being married to me. And what about our baby? Even if they leave it be, it will grow up being taught that its father was a traitor. Or worse, they might decide that no one with my blood can be allowed to live. That they're too much of a threat."

Stephania didn't want to think about that, although she also wasn't sure why Thanos's bloodline would be a threat. If she had decided to join in the condemnation of him, she had no doubt that the child would have been welcomed, simply because of its obvious nobility. Now, though… now, things would be more complicated.

"None of that is going to matter," Stephania said. "Because we're going to get you out of here."

That seemed to get an even bigger look of surprise than the fact that she was pregnant.

"What? How? Stephania, you can't take that much of a risk!"

129

Stephania shrugged. "It's a better risk than the risk of not having you, and it's already done. I've bribed the people I needed to bribe, and my maids will be putting sleeping draughts in the beer of any guards along the way."

Although what she'd smeared on her necklace hadn't been a sleeping draught. She hadn't had anything that gentle at hand, and she hadn't been willing to risk the guard going back on their deal. There was nothing, *nothing* she wouldn't do for Thanos.

"So you see," Stephania said, "I'm committed. They'll kill us both if they catch us now."

"I won't let that happen," Thanos said, and Stephania smiled at the thought that even here, even now, he wanted to protect her.

"*I* won't let that happen," Stephania corrected him. She held out her hand. "We have to hurry though."

She felt Thanos's hand slide into his. He looked so strong like that, and she passed him a short dagger.

"Just in case," she said.

Thanos looked at it and nodded. Stephania could see the determination there.

"Are you sure we'll be able to get out of here?" he asked.

Stephania kissed him. "Trust me. You're good at fighting those who need fighting. I'm good at… arranging things."

Maybe one day she would even be able to tell him about some of the things she'd arranged to keep him safe. Then again, maybe not. Thanos might have helped the rebels, but in some ways he was too pure, too innocent, for the things Stephania had done to protect him.

"We'll need to get out of the castle," Thanos said. "After that… I don't know. Perhaps the rebellion will have a way out of the city. If we can find them, maybe—"

"It's all right," Stephania said, cutting him off with a kiss. "I have this covered."

She led the way up through the dungeons, pulling Thanos along past the spots where there were screams or people crammed in together. She knew her husband would want to save them, but right then, that would only attract attention. And if others had to suffer so that the people she loved would be safe, Stephania didn't care.

She found guards slumped here and there. Her maids had done their jobs. She thought she glimpsed the body of the royal guard off to one side, but there was no time to check. They'd already spent too long there.

"We'll get out of here and head for the docks," Stephania said. "There will be a boat there waiting for us. After that... we'll find somewhere to go."

"Haylon," Thanos said. "We'll be safe on Haylon."

Perhaps, or perhaps Stephania would be able to think of somewhere better. The important part was that they would be together.

All they needed to do now was reach the docks.

CHAPTER TWENTY FIVE

Ceres didn't know the route that the rebel led her along. She traced her hand along the stone of the walls, feeling the strangeness of it. That strangeness, more than anything, told her how long she'd been away from the rebellion. So did the fact that Anka was now leader of the rebellion. It seemed like too much for the former slave to be running, because it seemed like too much for anyone to run by themselves.

In the passages and hidden spaces the rebels had carved out, Ceres saw more people than she could have believed. There were people training and working, laughing and sleeping. There were storerooms and workrooms, hallways and forges…

"Who all is leading you now?" Ceres asked as they walked.

"Besides Anka?" the rebel replied. Ceres could hear the respect there. From the moment she'd announced herself, he'd been as deferential as he might have been with a returning hero. "There's Edrin and Hannah, Berin and Sartes and—"

Ceres didn't listen beyond that. In that moment, none of the rest of it mattered.

"My father and my brother are here? Now? Take me to them!"

He led her to one of the sleeping spaces near the forges, and Ceres heart soared as she saw her father, sitting near a small bed—and her brother beside him.

"Father? Sartes?"

Her father looked up as though he'd seen a ghost. He paled, seeming overcome with disbelief, joy, relief. He stood there staring, as if not daring to hope that this might really be happening.

Ceres could understand the feeling. She felt equally shocked, and elated.

She saw Sartes sit up in the bed and clamber from it, rubbing sleep from his eyes.

"Ceres?" he said, and he sounded as shocked as her father looked. "You're alive?"

He stood there as though not knowing what to do, looking her up and down as though trying to make sure that it was really her, and not some imposter.

Ceres looked him up and down, trying to guess at all that had happened to him in the time she'd been away, but right then, she was just glad he was there. She opened her arms wide, and her brother ran to her, holding onto her tightly. He was a little taller than Ceres remembered, and stronger, too.

132

"You're *alive*!" Sartes said.

"We thought you were dead," her father said, moving to join in the hug. "I thought... I thought we'd lost you."

Ceres could hear notes of old grief there. She clung to them then, wanting to reassure them both that this was real.

"I've missed you both so much."

It seemed then as if the moment might never end. Certainly, Ceres didn't want it to.

"Where have you been?" her father asked. "What happened to you?"

"I washed up on an island," Ceres said. "There were people there who helped me to learn a lot of things about myself."

Her father's look changed a little. "What kind of things?"

"They taught me more about the power inside me," Ceres said. "And they led me to my mother."

This time, she saw Sartes frown. "Your mother? But our mother—"

Ceres put a hand on his arm. "Is still your mother, but not mine."

"You mean we're not family?" Sartes said. There was surprise there, but also a kind of fragility Ceres never wanted to hear in her brother.

Ceres hugged him again. "We will *always* be family, little brother, no matter who my parents turn out to be."

Her father held her at arm's length. "What did you think of your mother?"

Ceres thought for a moment or two. "She was... strange. Beautiful. Kind. I liked her, but she also seemed... sad. It must be hard for her, alone on the Island Beyond the Mist. How did you meet her?"

Her father shook his head. "That's a story for another time. What matters now is that you're here. It's *all* that matters."

"Are you with the army that's come?" Sartes said. "We can't find out what's happened."

Ceres smiled. "I'm *leading* the army. And we're going to take Delos from the Empire."

"I'd like to hear how you plan on doing that," Anka said from the doorway.

Ceres looked around at her, pausing as she saw her. She'd heard that Anka was in charge, but it was a very different thing to see it. She stood there, watching the way people reacted to her, seeing that it really was true.

133

Anka looked different from how she had in the slaver's cage. Different even from how she'd looked in the courtyard of the castle. Ceres could see the worry etched in her features, but also the sense of strength there.

Ceres hurried and they embraced. She could feel the strength in Anka's arms and shoulders.

"It's good to see you again. It looks as though you're doing a bit more than just holding things together now."

Anka spread her hands. "It turns out I had a talent for it, and I've had a lot of help. Sartes has done a lot. And of course, I would never be alive if it weren't for you."

They shared a look of mutual admiration.

Anka led them all away from the space by the forge through to a larger spot that had probably once been a storeroom, but was now filled with people.

Ceres could hardly believe how large the rebel army was now.

"Anka?" a woman asked. Ceres recognized her as Hannah, who'd been with the rebellion from the start. "Is that…Ceres? How is she alive?"

Ceres waited while Anka walked into the middle of the room, following her into a clear space there and letting her speak. Ceres could feel the way that people were looking at her. They knew who she was. They'd seen her in the Stade, or they'd heard about her role in the army.

"Those of you who've been in the rebellion long enough will recognize Ceres," Anka said. "Maybe some of the rest of you will as well. She fought in the Stade, and she is the reason why many of us are still here today."

Anka gestured for Ceres to step forward.

She did so, feeling the weight of the many eyes upon her. Most of these people would know who she was, some would even know her, but many wouldn't.

"I'm guessing that you have heard about the army besieging the city." She took a breath. "I am leading it."

Gasps arose from the crowd.

"You've brought an army to attack our city?" a man asked Anka.

She could see their confusion.

"We are not trying to destroy the city or hurt its people," Ceres said. "I've brought an army to *help* the rebellion."

"And how do we know that?" someone called from the crowd. "I saw the banners out there. Those are Lord West's men. Why would a lord help the likes of us, common peasants?"

"Because he hates the way the Empire rules," Ceres explained. "He just needed the right prodding to rise up against it."

"And we're supposed to believe that?" Hannah asked. "For all we know, he's just planning to replace the king with himself, and nothing will change. He could be duping you, Ceres."

"*Everything* will change," Ceres said. "And even if you don't trust Lord West, trust me."

"It's not about trusting you," Edrin said. "It's—"

"It's about trying to *win*!" Anka said. "Listen to yourselves. You're so worried about what might come next that you're not paying attention to what's happening now. We have a chance to crush the heart of the Empire. We have to take it. I trust Ceres. We should listen to what she has to say."

Ceres looked around at the people there.

"I understand that you're scared. You've been working for the overthrow of the Empire, but even so, this must feel like a huge step. I'm asking you to make the stand you've been preparing for. I'm asking you to take a big risk. I know that."

She waited for a moment or two, letting it sink in.

"But there comes a time when you have to stop preparing and *act*," she continued. "We have a chance to take Delos, but that chance will pass far too quickly. I have an army waiting out there, but when the rest of the Empire's forces get here, it will be caught between them and the city. If we attack the walls, we'll be slaughtered. But if we can take the city quickly, we can hold it against anyone."

"So you want us to do all the fighting for you?" one of the combatlords there asked.

Ceres shook her head. "You know me better than that. You've trained beside me, haven't you?"

The combatlord admitted: "You didn't shy away from the fights in the Stade."

"And I'm not going to run from this one," Ceres said. "I don't want you to win the city for me. I want us to win it together. My army can't get into the city, so I want us to open a gate where they can get inside without being cut to pieces. You wouldn't be fighting the whole of the Empire, just a few guards."

All of them fell silent. She understood. Someone would have to volunteer for the risky assignment of emerging from these tunnels and seeking out the least-guarded gate. It was a life and death task, and no one wanted it.

"I shall do it," came a voice.

Ceres turned, and her heart fell to see Sartes, standing there proudly.

"I can find the least defended gate," he said. "I'm the best placed to do it. No one would suspect me."

Ceres felt a wave of pride and fear for her brother. She didn't want to put her brother in danger, but no one else had volunteered. And he had a point.

"Sartes is right," Anka said. "And he is brave." She then turned to the crowd. "Will you be as brave? Once we find this gate, will you open it for Ceres and her army?"

A silence lingered, as a few nodded.

"And then you shall storm in?" Edrin asked.

Ceres nodded.

"And then we fight together," Ceres said. "Together, we can do this. Together, we can take Delos. Together, we can overwhelm the Empire and hold the city against the world. Together, we can forge a new world, but only if we do this now. Are you with me?"

There was silence, but that silence was quickly broken by a low chanting. Sartes started it, but the others soon took it up, one word rising until it filled the room.

"Ceres! Ceres!"

CHAPTER TWENTY SIX

Sartes moved carefully through the city streets in the hour before the dawn. He was watchful as he darted from doorway to alley mouth, clambered up stacked pallets, and blended in as best he could with those people who were out on the streets in spite of the early hour.

This being Delos, there were more than a few of those. It didn't matter that there was an army outside the city; its business still had to go on. That meant fishermen and merchants rising early to catch the tide out of the docks. It meant traders and food sellers setting up their stalls in the streets. It meant the night people coming back from whatever jobs they'd been doing by starlight, legal or otherwise.

It meant guards too, which was why Sartes was being careful. The Empire hadn't tried to impose a curfew on the city, presumably because everyone knew it would be unworkable, but Sartes still couldn't afford to be seen too openly. There was too much of a chance that someone might recognize him from the army, and then he would be taken as a deserter or a rebel.

Even so, he had better odds than most of the rebellion, which was why he was the one doing this. To any guard who *didn't* recognize him, Sartes would just look like an urchin worth no more attention than it took to kick him out of the way, or perhaps like an apprentice late to start work in his master's shop. Either way, it was easy enough to blend in with the people around him, to keep moving, making his way toward the city's gates.

Ceres undoubtedly had a harder job. While Sartes got to walk along safe streets, she had the job of sneaking back out to her waiting army to direct their attack. Sartes didn't want to think about the danger his sister might be in. He knew that she was a great fighter, but right then, one mistake and she would find herself facing the whole of the army within the city alone.

He couldn't do anything to help her, though. He just had to trust her, and make sure that he did his part.

He walked in the direction of one of the smaller gates first, the Dead Gate, where bodies were taken out on their way to the burial grounds. He ducked in behind a water butt while he watched the guards there. Too many, but more than that, the ground in front of the gate was too open. The guards would see any attack coming, and that would make it harder to succeed. No, he needed a better—

"Hey, what are you doing there, boy?" a guard demanded.

Sartes thought about running, but running would only prove that he was doing something wrong. He thought about the knife strapped to the small of his back, but that was a last resort. Sartes looked up at the guard, looking for any spark of recognition. That *would* have him reaching for the knife, because at that point, it would be the only way he lived.

"I... I'm sorry," Sartes said, thinking quickly. "I just thought if I could get close to the walls, I might be able to see the army. My friend Julin said that there were horsemen as far as the eye could see, and I wanted to look for myself, because I think he's lying."

The guard shook his head. "He's not lying."

"Could I... could I get up on the wall and see them?" Sartes said. It would let him see more of the defenses, and perhaps pick out the right spot to attack.

"No, you can't," the guard snapped back. "Do you think I'm running some kind of tour here, boy?"

"I'm just—" Sartes didn't have to fake his fear, although the guard probably wouldn't guess the reason for it. "We're going to be safe, aren't we? I mean, they aren't going to get in and kill us all, are they?"

"Don't be stupid, boy," the guard said. "Our walls are high, they aren't equipped for a siege, and the gates are strong. Why, the dockside gate is so well defended that half a dozen men can defend it, firing bolts through the murder holes until reinforcements arrive."

It seemed that Sartes had his gate, but he needed to be sure. He'd have to see it for himself.

"You should run along. A boy like you probably has chores to get to."

"Yes, sir," Sartes said, and ran, exactly as the soldier had commanded.

Perhaps it was because he was moving so fast that he got the sense that someone was following him. He was moving far faster than the crowds now, running from hiding place to hiding place because there was no time to waste. But there was someone else moving as fast. Sartes caught glimpses of them, or at least of the disturbances in the crowd behind him. He saw people moving out of the way of someone moving too quickly. He heard the beginnings of an argument, quickly cut off. On a stretch of cobbles, he thought he heard the slap of a pair of hobnailed boots.

Sartes headed for a deeper patch of crowd, householders and servants out looking for bread and meat even before it got fully light. He followed the flow of the crowd, forcing himself to wait even though there wasn't much more time for his scouting mission to continue. He thought he caught sight of a dark cloak as someone slipped through the crowd, obviously looking for him.

Sartes moved away carefully, waiting until he was well clear of the crowd before he started running again. He couldn't afford to waste time now. He had to check the gate and get back to the others. They were relying on him. *Ceres* was relying on him.

He sprinted to the dock district, sticking to the back streets and keeping his ears pricked for any continued pursuit. When he got to the dock gate, he looked around for a hiding spot and settled in on the fringes of a group of porters, obviously waiting for a ship that needed loading. They didn't seem to care about him. Possibly they thought he was waiting for the chance of easy coin like the rest of them.

Sartes watched the dockside gate. The guard he'd met had been right: there were almost no soldiers there. There didn't need to be, because the gates there were massive, solidly built with a portcullis behind them. There were stone towers above, crenulated on top, with a small catapult set there where it could do damage to anyone attacking. There was an alarm bell too, and Sartes guessed that it would summon soldiers from all across the district.

But there were ways to deal with it. What had once been clear routes to let the guards see threats coming were now cluttered with crates and sacks, ropes and barrels ready for loading or moving to warehouses. All of it would provide cover for the rebellion as its people moved closer. If they disguised themselves as dock workers, they might even be able to sneak right up to the guards before they attacked. They might be able to take the gate without losing anyone.

And then they would be able to let the army in. Sartes was a little nervous about that in spite of everything Ceres had said. He'd seen what armies were like when he'd been a conscript. Possibly Lord West's men would be more disciplined, and he knew that Ceres would never allow the kind of wanton destruction the Empire sanctioned, but even so, there would be violence. People would get hurt.

"It will be worth it," Sartes told himself. When they took the castle and brought down the king, it would be worth it. "Think of all the fighting it will stop."

Potentially, it could stop a wider war. The Empire's army attacked because the royals told it to. Take away the king and his cronies, and the army had no one to command it. From what Sartes had seen, half the men in it would desert at once, while the others would be cautious about fighting on for a lost cause. At a stroke, they could end this.

This was the gate. Sartes could feel it, just as he could feel the excitement building in him at the thought of what was going to happen next. They could do this. They could really do this.

First, though, he had to get back to the others, and he had to hurry, because dawn was coming far too fast.

Sartes ran back through the city's streets, over cobbles and dirt, gravel surfaces and evenly laid stone. Hardly anyone gave him a second glance. He saw a gang of slaves in the street, repairing a patch of broken cobbles under the supervision of armed guards. It was enough to remind him that no matter what happened in the attack, people would be better off. This was the only way to really change things in the Empire.

Sartes tried to imagine what it would be like once the Empire was gone. It was hard to think that far ahead. They'd all spent so long now working for it, but Sartes almost hadn't dared to think past the rebellion to what might lie beyond it. He'd been thinking perhaps that there would be time with his father, time for a normal life. Now, with Ceres back, he was already thinking of how much better things might be.

Ahead, he could see the entryway to the rebellion's tunnels, disguised as a half-forgotten stairway, hidden behind an overgrown arch. He crouched there, making sure that the coast was clear.

The others would be as excited to hear about the gate as he was to have found it. Anka would be pleased that she'd sent him, and grateful to know that she could trust him. The others would gain hope from it, because he'd given them the ideas that had worked in the burial grounds, and the Stade. His father would be proud of him, and Ceres—

Sartes caught a flicker of movement and half turned, but he was too slow. He just had time to see the cloaked figure running toward him before it slammed into him, sending the two of them tumbling to the ground in a scrambling sprawl of limbs.

Sartes twisted, reaching down to the small of his back for the knife he'd hidden there. Nothing was going to stop him from getting back to the rebellion now. His hand closed around the hilt and he drew it, but it seemed that his attacker had been expecting the move, because Sartes found the weight of a shin bearing down on his forearm, hard enough to make him cry out. A brutal twist of his wrist later, and the knife was skittering off across the cobbles.

Sartes hit out with his free hand but the figure grabbed his free wrist, using it to lever him over onto his belly, where Sartes quickly found his wrists bound with loops of cord. He tried to cry out, and tasted cloth as a rag was stuffed into his mouth.

"Lady Stephania sends her regards."

CHAPTER TWENTY SEVEN

From the top of the tenement building, Anka watched the rising sun, tracking its progress with growing trepidation. Across from her, she could see Berin, his fingers tightening on the forge hammer he held. Anka could understand it far too easily.

"Sartes should have been back by now," she said, although she said it softly. She didn't want the others there to see how nervous she was right then. Far too many of them were new recruits, who needed to believe that their leader knew what was going on if they were going to do this.

"He should," Berin agreed. "But Sartes is resourceful. He survived the worst the army could throw at him."

To Anka, it sounded like a man trying to convince himself, and Anka wasn't going to puncture it with too much reality if she didn't have to. For one thing, she hoped that the old smith was right. She didn't want to think about the possibility of Sartes being lost to them.

"We helped him then," she said, "and we'll help him now if he needs it. But probably, he doesn't. He's probably just holed up somewhere because he can't get back. Or he's still looking for the right opportunity."

Or he was dead or captured, having been caught by the soldiers Anka had sent him to spy on. If that proved to be the case, she wasn't sure that she would be able to forgive herself. Sartes was so eager to help sometimes that it was easy to forget that he was just a boy.

"He wants to do this," Berin said, as if guessing Anka's thoughts. "You didn't make him do it, and you know he's the best choice for it."

Anka guessed that was his way of saying that he didn't blame her. Anka would rather that Sartes was safe, though, and that there was nothing to blame her for.

"What do we do now?" Berin asked.

Anka shrugged. "We wait as long as we can for Sartes to come back. After that... I don't know. We think of something."

"Ceres is relying on us," Berin said.

Anka nodded. "And we're relying on her. A lot of things have to go right today."

And already, they were starting to go wrong. Sartes really should have been back by now with details of the best gate to target and the best way to go about their attack. He'd proven so effective in the past, providing them with the idea to take the Stade and the one to free the conscripts. Anka had come to rely on him as much as anyone.

Yet now, with the sun almost fully up, he wasn't there. Anka didn't know what to make of it.

Oreth came in, his knives strapped into place and a leather jerkin thrown on over his normal clothes. He looked ready for war, almost impatient for it.

"Do we know yet?" he asked.

Anka shook her head.

"Well," she heard him say, "we need to know soon. The combatlords are getting restless. So are the mercenaries Yeralt hired."

Either one would have been a problem. Both together were something more than that. The combatlords were strong, tough men, but they didn't take orders well. They were too used to fighting on their own terms against a single opponent, and cautious battle tactics were something that just didn't come into it. They would fight as long as they respected the people they were fighting for, and being kept waiting was not something they liked.

The mercenaries were a little more disciplined, but they didn't have the same commitment to the cause. Yeralt might believe they would stay there as long as they were paid, but Anka knew better. Mercenaries would only stay as long as they believed that there was a good chance of winning. They needed to believe that their commander was competent, or they would start to desert, or worse.

"We need to hurry," Oreth said. "If we hit them while they're changing guards, it will be twice as difficult."

Anka knew it was true, but there had to be a way.

"Ask around. Ask if anyone else has information on the gates. We can't wait for Sartes."

She saw Oreth nod. "I'll try to be discreet."

The wait was the hardest part. Every moment, Anka could see the sun rising higher. It was getting late. Maybe too late.

When Oreth returned, it was with a man who looked more like a beggar than one of the usual members of the rebellion. Anka didn't know his name, but that was far too common these days. He was probably one of the ones they'd brought into their rebellion in the last few days.

"This is Ralk," Oreth said. "Ralk, tell Anka what you told me."

"I've seen all kinds of things the last day or two," the beggar said. "Including which gates they're pulling men from to protect the others. There's a gate on the east side that we could take."

"You're sure?" Anka asked.

"I'm sure," Ralk replied. "It might be hard to get there, but once you're there…"

Anka wished she had more information, but forced herself to look confident. It was part of what being a leader *meant*. "We knew that wherever we attacked, it wouldn't be easy, so let's do it."

She led the way down into the tenement, where her people were waiting for her. She could feel the mixture of nerves and eagerness there in the habitual sharpening of weapons, the constant movement to no purpose.

She had to be clear now. "You all know why we're here. We're going to end this. We're going to open the eastern gate."

That got a cheer from some of those there. Others had the set faces of men and women who knew about the violence that would be coming.

"We'll go out in two waves," Anka said. "I'll lead the first wave, and Oreth will lead the second. The job of those of us in the first wave will be to take the guards on the gate by surprise and get it open. The second wave will come in after that to hold the gate until Ceres's army can arrive, rising up in the city to take it. The element of surprise is crucial here, so keep weapons out of sight until we're ready to act. Does everyone know what they need to do?"

Anka went through the room, picking out the people she needed. She picked some of the core of the rebellion, but also plenty of combatlords and mercenaries. This was a job for fighters. She checked their disguises like a mother ensuring her children were wrapped up against the cold, then headed out into the streets with them at her back. Berin was beside her, and Anka could see the head of his forge hammer in the palm of his hand, the haft hidden away up the sleeve of a long coat.

There were enough people in the streets that they could just about pass for the normal flow of the crowd. Even so, Anka could see people hurrying back inside their homes, shutting their doors as the rebellion passed. That was probably a good thing. The fewer people there were in the street, the less chance there was of ordinary people being hurt.

They walked in the direction of the gates, down through the poor districts and the merchant districts, keeping to the back streets and keeping their weapons out of sight. Anka held her breath as

144

they walked past a squad of guards loitering at the side of a street, yet they didn't give the rebels a second look, and Anka didn't order her people to attack. There was no need, and the worst thing they could do right then would be to get caught up in fighting in the streets. Even with the hundreds, the thousands who would rise behind them, they couldn't afford to give away what they were doing.

She looked up to see more of her people following across the rooftops, making their way over flat roofs and between gaps. She hoped that no one else would dare to look up then, because if they did, it was over. It would be open fighting, and the task of opening the main gates would be many times harder.

Anka signaled for the figures above to keep lower, and Oreth signaled back before slipping out of sight behind a roof edge. She kept going, making her way along the roads that skirted the city's east-west processional way. That, more than anything, convinced her that the gate was the right one to try for. With it open, Ceres's forces would be able to ride down the broad expanse of the street almost all of the way to the castle. The invasion of the city would be over almost before anyone knew what was happening.

In the distance now, Anka could see the gates. They were imposing things, covered in metal, embossed with scenes of the Empire's triumph. The stone bastions around them were solid enough that siege engines would probably barely scratch them. The walls were high and strong, with watchers set every hundred paces or so.

Yet Ralk had been right: there wasn't a whole army there on the walls. Those soldiers there were seemed to be loitering in the space in front of the gates, waiting for any move from beyond the walls. That made sense to Anka. They couldn't stand at full readiness all the time. Of course they would wait there until there was some sign of threat. The trick would be to get the gates open before they realized that there was anything wrong.

"We'll go in pretending to be a group of disgruntled traders," Anka said, keeping her eyes on the gates. "If we make enough noise about it, the soldiers will be too busy arguing with us to see the real threat."

"Or they might decide to attack to teach us a lesson," Berin pointed out.

"If that happens, Oreth will bring his group in to back us up," Anka assured him. By now, she knew how the other members of the rebellion would react. "Either way, it will look like a scuffle rather than a real attack. Half of them won't bother joining in until it's too late."

She turned back to the others. She could see the nerves there. Several of the newer members of the group were fingering their hidden weapons, obviously ready for action.

"Stay calm," Anka said. "And keep those blades hidden until I make my move. When we go up there, we're just slightly stupid traders who want to know why a little thing like an army is getting in the way of us getting to make our living, all right? We're going to go up and demand that they open the gates for us. If we're really lucky, they might even let us do it, just so that they can think about shutting us outside. Is everybody ready?"

Anka saw the members of her little group nodding to one another. The mercenaries crowded to the back, but that was only to be expected with their sort.

"Then let's go," she said, turning back to the gate. She waved to where she thought Oreth was waiting above, but there was no response.

Anka looked around for him, because this needed to be coordinated, but there was no sign of him. She kept going anyway, because it was too late for anything else, and it was only as she set off that she saw the one thing she'd hoped not to see: figures struggling on the rooftop. Oreth was fighting against a pair of figures, silhouetted against the morning sun. She saw the flash of a blade as it plunged into him.

It was only as she saw that the figures were wearing the colors of the rebellion that Anka understood.

She heard the snick of blades clearing scabbards. Instantly, she spun back, but it was already too late. She saw her people there in the hundreds, and the mercenaries, the new recruits, had them. Berin had a blade pressed to his throat. One of the combatlords was on his knees, blood pouring from a wound. Three mercenaries had swords leveled at Anka.

She tried to think of something to do, something to say, but there was nothing. She'd warned the others about the dangers, and now it had come to pass.

They'd been betrayed.

CHAPTER TWENTY EIGHT

Thanos looked back over Delos as he rode down toward the docks, tension there with every stride of the creature as the dawn rose. At any moment, he expected to see guards appearing behind them, riding him and Stephania down.

"It will be all right," Stephania said from beside him. "By the time they realize that you've escaped, we'll be long gone."

Thanos nodded. Stephania knew him better than he could have believed.

"It's strange to think this might be the last time we see Delos," Thanos said, looking back at the city. In spite of the squalor of the docks, the destitution of the city, it was still difficult to be leaving it like this.

"It doesn't matter," Stephania said, reaching out for his hand without slowing down. "So long as we're together."

It did matter, though. It didn't feel right that because of the evil of the Empire, he and his wife were being forced to flee the place where they'd been planning to build their lives.

"Do you really think they'll take us in on Haylon?" Stephania asked him.

Thanos nodded, trying to look confident in spite of the argument he'd had with Akila. "When they hear what's happened, they'll help us."

They had to. It was the only place they had left to go. Now that the Empire had condemned him, surely that would be enough to prove to the rebels that he was on their side.

"And we'll be stuck on an island that's under attack," Stephania pointed out.

Thanos wanted to reassure her. He wanted to make things so much better for her. "Haylon is beautiful," he said. "The Empire can't touch us there, and it doesn't have to be forever. Sooner or later, the Empire will fall, and we'll be able to go anywhere we want. You, me, and our child."

"Just you, me, and our child," Stephania said. Thanos saw her smile. "Put that way, I think we'll be fine wherever we go. We need to hurry though. This captain will carry us for coin, but the boat won't wait long."

They rode to the docks as quickly as they dared. Ahead, Thanos could see a boat waiting. It wasn't as large or grand as some of the galleys the Empire used, but it had the sleek look of a ship well used to keeping ahead of pursuers.

"A smuggling boat?" Thanos said, as they got closer.

"I've always tried to find friends in strange places," Stephania replied.

Thanos dismounted and helped her down. He slapped the rumps of their horses, setting them running. The more he and Stephania could disguise their trail, the better it would be, for them and for anyone who had helped them.

They stepped toward the waiting boat, and it was only then that Thanos saw the figure slip from the shadow of a stack of crates. He carried the markings of a royal messenger, and he thrust a scroll into Thanos's hand, and then did not wait as he turned to go.

"From Lucious, my lord," he said. "You may want to open it."

And without another word, he hurried off, disappearing into the darkness.

Thanos stared at Stephania, who stared back at him, each of them floored. Lucious knew they were here; and yet he had not come. He could have had them imprisoned if he'd wanted. Then why hadn't he? Thanos wondered. And then he realized there could only be one reason: whatever was in this scroll was so damaging, he did not have to appear.

That, and perhaps because Thanos would kill him on the spot.

Thanos studied the scroll with a new interest. It was genuine, the messenger was genuine, and the wax seal was genuine. It was definitely from Lucious.

"What are you doing?" Stephania asked, examining it with disgust. "Who cares what that beast has to say? Discard it at once!"

But Thanos shook his head.

"No, my lady," he said. "We must know what he knows before we embark. This vessel, after all, may be a trap."

He looked back up at the smuggling ship, the hardened faces of its men, now unsure of anything.

Slowly, Thanos broke the seal, his heart pounding, bracing himself as he did. He read aloud, so Stephania could hear.

Thanos,

I would have come myself. But if I bring you back, then there's always a chance you could talk your way back into the king's good graces. So I believe this scroll shall suffice to serve my purpose.

I hear things now, brother. And I thought you might like to hear some of them before you leave. If you choose to leave.

Ceres is alive.

Thanos lowered the scroll, his heart slamming, disbelieving, trying to process what he was reading. His world reeled at the news, and he felt it spinning out from under him.

Ceres was alive? Thanos's heart leapt at the prospect, but he didn't dare to believe it. Not when it was Lucious saying it.

He continued reading:

If you don't believe it, ask your lovely wife. She knows all about what happened to Ceres. After all, she was the one who arranged for Ceres to be sent to the Isle of Prisoners.

Thanos looked up at Stephania, expecting to see her deny it, but instead, her face was reddening.

His heart dropped at her expression.

Could it be possible?

"Stephania?" he asked, his heart broken.

"I... she would have been dead in the Stade if I hadn't," Stephania said. "I saved her."

Now Thanos reddened. He could hardly believe his ears.

"No more!" Stephania cried. "Read no more!"

She reached out, as if to rend the scroll, but Thanos, intrigued, pulled it back and read fervently.

But this should come as no surprise. Stephania, after all, is the one who arranged to have you killed. Who do you think hired the Typhoon?

Thanos turned back to Stephania, expecting her to tell him that it was all lies. Instead, she just stood there, looking torn, looking guilty.

"Stephania?" Thanos said.

"I... I don't want to start off our new life together by lying to you," Stephania said. "I love you, Thanos. I never thought I could love anyone like I love you."

"What are you saying?" Thanos asked, feeling his world melting around him.

Suddenly, she burst into tears, rushing in to hug him.

"You were supposed to be mine," Stephania said. "You said it yourself. You cast me aside for her, for Ceres. So I sent a message to the Typhoon. If I couldn't have you—"

She wept and wept.

"I know how it sounds. It was awful. I should never have done it. I just couldn't bear the thought of losing you. And I didn't love you then like I do now. I am so ashamed of it. Please believe me. So ashamed. I beg God every day for forgiveness. I am begging for your forgiveness. Now, I would give my *life* for yours."

Thanos couldn't believe what he was hearing. He stared at Stephania as though only just seeing her for the first time. Perhaps he was.

"It was *you* who tried to have me killed," he said, incredulous. His voice sounded flat, even to himself. It felt right then as if his emotions hadn't caught up with the rest of him. "*You*. The woman I love most of all. The only one in this court I trusted."

"I love you, Thanos," she said through her tears. "I've loved you even when I didn't know what love was."

He didn't know what to think right then, what to feel. Ceres was alive, and Stephania had tried to kill him. She had tried to kill Ceres, too.

And yet Stephania was pregnant with his child, she claimed to love him, she'd married him. And she had risked her life to break him out of jail.

But she'd also tried to have him killed, and she'd sent Ceres away to die. He should have felt angry, but instead, he simply felt as though the world had been turned on its head. He didn't know what to feel.

How could he ever trust her? How could he ever know who Stephania truly was? Did she even know who she was?

"You went around with me, looking for the killer," Thanos said. "You pointed me at Lucious. You led me to the stable boy and then you had him killed."

He could feel the anger rising up in him at that. Stephania had been willing to sacrifice innocents in her efforts to protect herself, and to blame Lucious.

Stephania reached out for his shoulder, and Thanos shook her off.

"No," he said. "I can't. I thought you loved me."

"I *do* love you," Stephania insisted. Thanos could see the tears in her eyes. The hard part was that he had no way of knowing if they were genuine now. He didn't want them to be, because even now, he couldn't bear the thought of Stephania in pain.

Thanos shook his head. "I don't think you know what love really means."

"I risked *everything* for you," Stephania said. "If that's not love, I don't know what is. I need to spend my life with you. I've *killed* people to keep you safe."

She wept and hugged him and he stood there, numb, not knowing what to say or think.

"I only tell you all this because I've changed," Stephania insisted. With the tears in her eyes, a part of Thanos wanted nothing more than to comfort her.

He reached out for her automatically, and he saw the hope in her eyes.

"I… I wouldn't have married you if I didn't love you, Stephania. But I still don't think you understand."

"I shouldn't have tried to kill you," Stephania wept softly.

She kissed him then, and Thanos could taste the sweetness of her lips as she did it. He wished that things could be this easy. Just kiss, and everything would be better. Just pretend that none of it had happened. He wished he could do that. Maybe it would hurt less then.

Finally, Thanos pulled away.

"Do you remember the name of the stable boy you had killed?" Thanos asked. "Do you remember the name of the isle to which you sent Ceres off to live a tortured life?"

Stephania paused, looking stricken. "What? I… Thanos, this is about us."

Thanos slowly shook his head.

He stepped toward the ship. When Stephania went to follow, he put a hand up to stop her.

His heart broke even as he did it. It was the hardest thing he'd ever had to do.

"I am sorry, Stephania," he said. "I have grown to love you. I truly have. And yet…I can't… I can't be with you after this. However much I want to."

"But Thanos, please, you can't—"

"No," Thanos said. He tried to keep his voice steady. "It's not even the fact that you tried to kill me. We could get past that. It's what you've done to everyone else."

"No one but you matters," Stephania said.

"Yes, they do," Thanos countered. "They matter as much as either of us. More sometimes. If you can't see that …"

Finally, Stephania's eyes squinted in a slow rage.

"You're going to find her, aren't you?" Stephania demanded, and Thanos could hear the anger there, the jealousy. "You're going to run back to her."

He hadn't thought that far ahead, but now, he knew he was.

"I do love you, Stephania," Thanos said. "But yes, I will find Ceres. I have to. I never left her. I had been told she was dead."

"They'll kill me if I stay here," Stephania said. He could hear the pleading note there. "They'll execute me. Thanos," she said, her voice sounding as though it might crack at any moment.

He knew she was right. They would. And that broke his heart most of all. Especially as she had just risked it all to save his life.

And yet, he could not be with her. Not anymore.

Thanos was already making his way onto the smugglers' vessel. He looked back and watched, with a broken heart, Stephania slump in place there, sobs wracking her body. It took everything Thanos had not to run back to her.

The captain met him on the deck, looking him over. Thanos saw him frown slightly.

"Where to?" the captain asked.

Thanos replied without looking back, his voice cold and hard and determined:

"The Isle of Prisoners."

The captain's eyes widened, whether in fear or awe, Thanos did not know.

"Get a move on, you dogs!" the captain called out to his crew. "Soldiers are coming. And I don't like soldiers! We need to be away from here."

Thanos stood there as the boat lurched into motion, slipping through the dock smoothly. He looked back at Delos, in what might be his last view of the city. It had been his home for so long, and now it felt like ashes to him. On the docks, getting smaller, he could see Stephania crumpled there.

She looked up and reached out for him, sobbing.

"THANOS!" she shrieked. "NO!"

He closed his eyes and heard her shriek rolling off the rising fog, and he knew it was a sound that would reverberate within him forever.

The only thing that made it bearable was the thought of what he might be sailing toward.

Ceres was alive out there.

And he would find her.

CHAPTER TWENTY NINE

Ceres sat atop her horse, watching the walls of the city as the sun rose. She forced herself to remain still, but her horse was skittish.

Something was wrong.

"Still no news from the other gates?" she asked Lord West.

The nobleman shook his head. "You will know as soon as there is a signal, I promise you."

"In the Stade, the waiting was always the worst part," Ceres said. "Listening to the fighting outside."

"Most of war is waiting," Lord West said. "Waiting, or camping in the rain, or marching through mud. When I was a young man like Gerant, I used to dream of glorious clashes and charges. No one tells you about the mud."

"Or the blood," Ceres said. "Or the death."

"You're too young to have seen so much," Lord West said.

"In Delos, I think there are plenty of people my age who have seen violence," Ceres pointed out.

"But none with the blood of the Ancient Ones," Lord West said. "And maybe this will change things." He looked as though he might say more, but he broke off, pointing. "Look there, below!"

Ceres followed the line of his finger, and she saw a gate opening at the side of the city. Not one of the largest gates, a merchant gate meant for moving goods in, but still more than big enough for what they wanted.

"They've done it," Ceres said. "The rebellion has given us our way in."

Lord West nodded, then yelled to his men. "Form up!"

Horns sounded, and the horsemen of the North Coast gathered together in a great wedge, their horses whickering as they held in place, obviously sensing some of what might come next.

"When you're ready, my lady," Lord West said, "just give the order."

Ceres paused, but not for long. She could only guess at the fighting that had to be taking place below as the rebellion struggled to hold the gate. Even if they'd managed to open it by stealth, there would still be guards coming to investigate soon. They had to act.

"For Delos," she called out. "Charge!"

She heeled her horse forward, and the riders of the North Coast went forward. Their wedge felt like an arrowhead now, fired by some great invisible bow toward the waiting roundel of the city.

There were so many of them there, but even so, they felt like one coordinated thing in that moment. One entity, following behind Ceres, matching her stride for stride.

She saw Gerant there, his spear flying his uncle's pennant. Around him were other young men, other pennants reflecting other nobles, but they were all following Ceres because of what she represented and what she wanted to achieve. Together, they thundered down toward the city, the sound of their hooves so loud that Ceres imagined the king being able to hear them in the castle.

Good, she thought, let him know what was coming for him.

They reached the open gates of the city, powering in through the wide space left there for goods and carts. Ceres had her sword in her hand then, fully expecting to find herself in the middle of a fight between the rebellion and the army. Yet as far as she could see, the streets beyond the gates were empty.

Something felt wrong again, but Ceres couldn't simply bring her horse to a halt. Not with so many men piling into the city behind her. Instead, she had to raise her hand to get them to slow, trying to call out over the sound of horseshoes on cobbles.

"Stop! Everybody stop! There's something wrong."

Lord West's men were well trained, but even so, it took them time to come to a halt. They swirled around in a great open space intended for merchants and their teams of oxen. Ceres knew it well. She'd been to it plenty of times with her father, and normally by this hour it was bustling with the sounds of people haggling and arguing, straining and trying to get animals to go the way they wanted.

Instead, it was so silent that Ceres could make out the cawing of the crows that had settled on one nearby rooftop.

"This is wrong," Ceres said, looking around. "There should be people here."

"Perhaps they fled indoors when the rebellion took the gates?" Gerant suggested.

"Then where are the rebels?" Ceres demanded. "They should be here."

"I agree," Lord West said, riding up beside her. "But we cannot let this chance pass for a feeling." He called out to his men. "Be on your guard."

They rode forward, and still, everything was too quiet. Unnaturally so. There had been more noise in some of the woodland they'd passed through on the way there. This had the carefully still silence of too many people making no sound.

Then they passed a side street, and Ceres saw the carts that had been brought up there, blocking the way. She heard the crows again, and this time they took to the air, scattering as someone moved near them.

"Back!" she yelled. "Back! It's an ambush!"

They'd been betrayed. That much was obvious, although Ceres didn't want to guess who had done it. The Empire had known they were coming though. More than that, they'd known enough of their plan to emulate it, and draw them into a trap that they couldn't resist.

"We need to get away!" Ceres called again. "Scatter. All of you, scatter!"

There were too many men, though, and too many horses. They crowded the square beyond the merchants' gate, filling it until it seemed impossible that they might be able to turn around. With the side streets blocked, they couldn't even flee that way, and half of the men seemed not to understand what was going on in any case.

Ceres leaned over to Gerant to order him to sound the retreat on his horn. To shout it if he couldn't do that. Anything that might get them out of the killing ground of the square. Even as she did it, though, she heard another horn sound, in a note that was deep and harsh, different from anything Lord West's men carried.

There was metallic crash as a portcullis came down across the merchants' gate. Above them, figures appeared in the armor of the Empire, armed with bows, slings, and javelins.

Feathers seemed to sprout from Gerant's open visor. For a moment, Ceres stared at him, unable to comprehend the oddity of it. Then she saw the rest of the arrow's haft, and she watched as the young nobleman tumbled slowly from the saddle.

She barely had time to look up as arrows darkened the sky, hundreds of them, thousands, as the Empire's men opened fire.

As she fell with the men all around her, one final thought ran through her mind:

So this is what death looks like.

COMING SOON!

Book #4in Of Crowns and Glory

Books by Morgan Rice

THE WAY OF STEEL
ONLY THE WORTHY (BOOK #1)

VAMPIRE, FALLEN
BEFORE DAWN (BOOK #1)

OF CROWNS AND GLORY
SLAVE, WARRIOR, QUEEN (BOOK #1)
ROGUE, PRISONER, PRINCESS (BOOK #2)
KNIGHT, HEIR, PRINCE (BOOK #3)
REBEL, PAWN, KING (BOOK #4)

KINGS AND SORCERERS
RISE OF THE DRAGONS
RISE OF THE VALIANT
THE WEIGHT OF HONOR
A FORGE OF VALOR
A REALM OF SHADOWS
NIGHT OF THE BOLD

THE SORCERER'S RING
A QUEST OF HEROES
A MARCH OF KINGS
A FATE OF DRAGONS
A CRY OF HONOR
A VOW OF GLORY
A CHARGE OF VALOR
A RITE OF SWORDS
A GRANT OF ARMS
A SKY OF SPELLS
A SEA OF SHIELDS
A REIGN OF STEEL
A LAND OF FIRE
A RULE OF QUEENS
AN OATH OF BROTHERS
A DREAM OF MORTALS
A JOUST OF KNIGHTS
THE GIFT OF BATTLE

THE SURVIVAL TRILOGY
ARENA ONE (Book #1)
ARENA TWO (Book #2)
ARENA THREE (Book #3)

About Morgan Rice

Morgan Rice is the #1 bestselling and USA Today bestselling author of the epic fantasy series THE SORCERER'S RING, comprising seventeen books; of the #1 bestselling series THE VAMPIRE JOURNALS, comprising twelve books; of the new vampire series VAMPIRE, FALLEN; of the #1 bestselling series THE SURVIVAL TRILOGY, a post-apocalyptic thriller comprising three books; of the #1 bestselling epic fantasy series KINGS AND SORCERERS, comprising six books; of the new epic fantasy series THE WAY OF STEEL; and of the new epic fantasy series OF CROWNS AND GLORY. Morgan's books are available in audio and print editions, and translations are available in over 25 languages.

Morgan loves to hear from you, so please feel free to visit www.morganricebooks.com to join the email list, receive a free book, receive free giveaways, download the free app, get the latest exclusive news, connect on Facebook and Twitter, and stay in touch!

CPSIA information can be obtained
at www.ICGtesting.com
Printed in the USA
LVHW022203291120
672984LV00067B/4244